the living room

GW00762150

PULP FACTION>60 ALEXANDER ROAD>LONDON>N19 3PQ
http://www.tecc.co.uk/twin/pulpfact
distributor>central books

British Library CIP data: The Living Room
I. Palmer, Elaine
823.0108 [FS]
ISBN:1899571027

Editor: Elaine Palmer
Assistant Editor: Robyn Conway
Art Editor: Daniel Mogford
Designers: Pearl Delaney, Michael Kowalski, Martin Black.
Distributors UK: Central Books 0181 986 4854
US: AK Press, San Francisco.
Advertising: Independent Spirit 251 2723
Original Artwork & Illustration: Andrew Stuart, Phil Julian, Adam j Maynard, Ralph Mepham, Robyn Conway, Frank Rynne.
Thanks to: Twin Media who run our web site at **http://www.tecc.co.uk/twin/pulpfact** London Arts Board, ChéRecords, the Paul Hamlyn Foundation, and all the writers who have sent work to Pulp Faction in the past year.

LONDON ARTS BOARD

Contents

Home Game

Fraser C. Addecott

Who do you support? The question flabbergasted me. What did it mean? Who did I support? I was dumbfounded; I no longer knew.

In Africa I had known everything there was to know — everything I needed to know. I knew that, every morning, the sun would rise over the acacia at the end of the garden into a huge cloudless sky. I knew that at three o'clock thunder and fantastic streaks of lightning would flash into the hills in the south sometimes igniting a tree, sometimes leading to to a full-scale bush-fire. Then, I knew, the rain would pour down solidly for an hour, only for it to cease just as suddenly, allowing the sun to burn even more strongly, making steam rise in clouds from the drying roads. I knew that if you found the edge of the thunderstorm, the air was so still that you could step in and out of the sheet of water like stepping in and out of a doorway. And I knew that if there was a rainbow it meant it was a monkey's wedding. I knew that if you chanced upon a lizard basking on a rock and chased it, it would shed its tail and leave it wriggling on the ground as it raced into hiding, while the dogs, fooled, snapped at the dying appendage.

When my father brought out his automatic rifle in the evening and we sat together on the verandah and dismantled it, and cleaned each part meticulously, and re-built it, then I knew that he had already been home for three months and that the next day he would dress in his camouflage uniform and disappear for three months. I knew that he had gone to fight the terrorists who were trying to steal our country, and that my mother would behave strangely for a few days, sometimes snapping at us kids, occasionally hugging us, and that the servants would keep out of her way. I knew that the servants were grateful to us for providing them with jobs in our home and garden, even though they had to live in the kia at the bottom of that garden and had only one weekend off every three months to visit their families. I knew that my mother spent more on the meat for the dogs than she did on the meat for the boys. But I knew that the house-boy liked me because he called me Little Boss (especially when my mother was around), and the garden-boy had taught me how to ride a bicycle.

I knew for a fact that in London it was always foggy, and the telephone boxes and double-decker buses were always red, and the taxis black, and that the people spoke either like the Queen or like Danny Kaye. I knew that Englishmen were always polite, and I knew that they had white men sweeping the streets.

But now, in a wet school playground, I knew nothing. In a cold, wet English school playground with no sun, no sky, no lizards and no rocks. With no father, standing proudly in camouflage uniform, with no dogs, no terrorists and no servants, I knew nothing. *Who do you support?* The boy's face was twisted, the words were accusing, threatening. My expression betrayed my incomprehension. His eyes blazed as he raised a clenched fist to display a blue and white striped scarf dangling from his wrist. *What team do you support!*

Football. It suddenly hit me. School holidays, the long, long drive south, the beach, the sea, the imported chocolate.

The hotel, watching the F.A. Cup final live from England in the hotel bar, and the men sitting on stools in their shorts, drinking beer from bottles and watching the girls go past in their bikinis, while the women were away shopping for the things we couldn't get at home. My father, drunk, slapping the waiter who had spilt the tray, *black bastard*; although I had seen my uncle knock the tray as he leapt to celebrate a goal. And Manchester United raising the cup.

Manchester United, I blurted. *I support Manchester United*. I was saved. I knew who I supported. The eyes stared at me, amazed, then the face sighed, the blue and white scarf flashed and the fist smashed into my eye. I hit the wet tarmac, and knew nothing.

PLaStic
Adam.j.Maynard.

The pink inflatable reindeer was grotesque but it offered a way back to early youth. Swimming pools, the shallow end, chlorine, bombing, shouting and screaming. It was dangerous to jump off the top board, but it had to be done. The shiny film that was the water's surface had to be broken. It would be cool to live on some farmstead somewhere. All chickens, pigs, and corn, Pea had thought, only seconds after she had entered the water. Imagine riding a real horse instead of the plastic one in the foyer of the swimming pool, imagine flying to exotic lands in a real aeroplane instead of the plastic one in the foyer of the swimming pool.

sundance terminal

jungle grab, gag, and lunge all through five
summers — hunting. hunting is hurting,
breathing is forbidden, birdsong is fingered
by torn sharks sullen on corners, so many
electric guitars now and no power left to
hunt. junk seems reasonable. electric guitars
dread truth. all candyfloss bleating things
soon form aspirations to express love.
in infancy everyone blossoms free and giant
explains how she conquered self hate. junk is
reasonable to those who feel like junk. everyone privately says yes in the middle of the
night. in daylight it has no meaning no more.
numbered in the hurricane too soon, maytime
springs up and over through to the new
hunting ground —the gaps betwen the junk
hunt.
god is slipping in the back door but we're
scared to turn the light on in case we
frighten him off again. i tried to escape my
territory, turn my back on fear shooting
blind crass big bullets at its tiny heart in
the bleachout dark all around i ran from the
hunt into sex and sanity. i ran away from
hunting god and ran into myself hiding in the
fresh grass under a hot fat sun where snake
nature cries mercy into the baleful haphazard
inscrutable eye of providence. TA DA ta ta-ta
ta ta ta-da. if my neck stretch long enough
down this pit of the fucked up past maybe
it'll goo like gum thinned with fingers and
stream out under the bewildering shit through
to the other sides out into the hot green sun
of love.
god wades junked and gutted across a dirty
beach. god stops at a beach stall to buy ice-
cream. god has found a pair of wraparound
shades and refuses to join a band.
he's back for real this time. you really feel

good about somebody go get them. then fire breathing
hopelust dawns puking into ashtrays, crying. breezes.
the sun never touched a cigarette i believe. i believe
splatted on the bumper of your smile. i believe getting
my soul screwed good. gas flowers, airship pass, big
fish through the sky when you stretch and yawn,
the curve of your neck, hot silky waist, breasts from
heaven. weird madness. called out the horsemen but they
were icecream vendors. too much has changed inside
keeps changing in front of my amazed zoom-bloated eyes.
shock and blind networks of thought, the slob of
boredom slunk into, jumped us from the loaded past gone
so why do we all spend so much time there?
now is here, real, we in landslide control. a free new-
bladed forest of raw flux after all the layers of
technoinformation overload burn away, show the world my
soul what else can i do? it slithers and chokes and
releases the world too.
no walls no dams no blinkers no frontiers no definition,
extremes come to the fore when everything gets vague and
unnameable. absurd escapist mickey mouse philosophies
replaced as quickly as they are hailed as the NEW IDEA.
you see it every day on a television somewhere.
the second coming is tv, brakes redundant, the runaway
flying tightrope slop of brooding over the edgeness,
here we go, when your worst fears seem the only thing
that could possibly be true, to have this, look it
blaring in the face, dream of the sixties dead and
burnt out, desperate bids to steer communities away
from the facts, so many people trying to grab time by
the spine and change something, but the only thing you
can change is yourself and those who know that can't do
it for themselves ha ha ahahaha.
enough clues now, it's just what you feared, IT IS YOUR
FEAR. small things all that are left for us, smallest
are tears and they do keep on flowing, a wet tired grin
of life, the shit and shine dancing in our little
hearts, look at it all. what can you do? i dunno. lost.
free. hungry. space. fan of lasers sweep ocean
horizons. lighthouses. set up at the edge of things
near the death of safety. craving what? pixilated
helium ships. making love. love. a morning that brings
all craving to an end. peace. fulfillment. no more

pressure at my temples. bliss. spock for pope.
to learn anything worth learning you have to go to
places for which there are no maps yet in existence and
have a look for yourself. the world... fuck it with
feverish kisses, grind it with my eyes, pump it deep
and long, give give give for now there is nothing left
to take. the snails are rutting and the breathtaking
amble of don't scream don't get uptight don't say i'm
wrong but don't say you're right halfway here and
halfway there nowhere here is better than unknown
there, she's my girl, wot's an affair? democracy is a
linoleum duck, webtoed and gawping, quacking when it's
poked with reality.
to let the day go by and by and bye-bye chocolate faced
world, all sorts engraved by journeymen, cars
possessing your soul, drink to catch your tears in,
fallow earth to sit and feel smug by, churches to peer
at the forgotten past, laserquests to peer at the
forgotten present, cinemas to peer at forgotten life
slipping away as we watch illusions of ourselves
fritter and fuck and fathom our lives for us in a dark
room full of comfy seats to let our power and lust and
passion diffuse harmlessly and above all WITHOUT FUSS,
quietly, numbing our arses so that our minds won't catch
on, dragging our cardboard hearts around a huge coil of
70mm plastic infused with ghosts from a stranger's
imagination, plugged into the switchboards of distraction,
BEING ENTERTAINED IN CASE WE MIGHT NEED IT.
show me your throat and i'll leave it stripped to the
freezing sunny dawn, feel the wind on your skin LIVE
AND GIVE YOUR FEAR TO THE NIGHT. THEEEE NIGHT, nightly,
nightly, naughty, nibbling, nana mouskori, nana land of
a million gerbils, agog, humping their lives into a
fury of spicy chicken dip. the sun the sea the air made
of razors.

martin messent

WE GOT DEEP

Amanda Gazidis

We got deep at the Deep-pan
pizza company,
You said the eyes are the
windows to the soul,
I thought that's cheap.
Why do you wanna go there?
It's barren as hell I swear.
I thought I'm lost for looking,
Implausibility cooking.
I'm going to the top, but
nowhere much,
Dead in fashion, but out of
touch.
We lost our souls
In a city of super-brow
schemes,
We'll find it yet if you stay
by me.
Do you want the pizza deep-
pan,
or not so deep and crispy?

the white trunk story

justin cooke

i first began my obsessive search for white swimming trunks back in 1991 in my first year of university. totally out of luck and in desperation i wrote to vogue. the editor, ms schulman, wrote back and confirmed the rarity of the desired garment. "the only designers i know," she wrote, "are homme (pronounced ohm), here is their italian telephone number..." i called them on the mercuryphone in my hall of residence. i used to think mercury were the coolest communicators on earth what with harry enfield and second by second billing. but then i found out that they were owned by cable and wireless and that they were withdrawing their public pay phone network. sure enough, all over london white stickers appeared on phone booths informing non mobile phone users of this fact. anyway, i get through to the swimwear department, "no i am sorry, those were underpants...we do not have any...click," and the call is neatly expiated. i sigh and accept that for now my search is over. then as if to rub salt into the wind, next month's vogue has a single page retrospective on men's swimwear with a picture of johnny w, the olympic swimmer who went on to play tarzan, in a pair of white swimming trunks.

ok, so they are passion killer trunks, but they are white and they are cool. now, unless johnny w was wearing pants, which was possible and something i have often thought of doing, this photo proves that someone must have made white swimming trunks at some point in the twentieth century. heartily and with my frustration decidedly dormant i resumed my quest through contemporary culture. two more years pass and we move luckless, to 1995. i am now an employed graduate in a state of positive debt (once paid my salary, i have enough space on my overdraft to spend until i have again reached my limit). one day, whilst searching in harrods' fifth floor department 'way in', my eyes catch a rack of women's swimwear. excitedly, i pick up the persil white bikini bottoms and place them nervously against my hips. but i know to wear them would be an ill-fitting compromise and i depart.

my next stop is covent garden tube. on arrival i am dumbstruck, positively flabbergasted: every single platform billboard is covered in glorious b&w images of armani men and women. slowly i dripfeed each one into my image bank and head towards the yellow 'way out' sign. suddenly it registers. there is a man wearing white pants. nope, he is not wearing white pants. he is wearing white swimming trunks. i erupt, flush and enter the life saving clothes store. the smile and greet girl at the door tells me that the swimwear collection will arrive in 2 weeks. with itchy feet, i re-enter the shop

14 days later and head straight for the brand new swimwear department. the swimwear assistant will not comprehend that i am looking for white swimming trunks, "no we have only these," he smirks in crazed disbelief. it is true, there are no white trunks in the store. perhaps i hallucinated the picture in covent garden with the black band above the photo saying, 'swimwear', maybe it just said 'underwear'?

victim of a fashion mirage? surely not. i know i am sad, but not mad. the following saturday i see the poster again, i check my head and it definitely says 'swimwear'. i go to the store again and a woman in the basement confirms that there are no white trunks. "yes there are," i say trying to retain a poise of cool indifference. but it is no good, my voice gives out that saturday shopper manic hoarse pitch change mid-sentence. she looks and i glare into the catalogue and show her the photograph, minus the title 'swimwear'. oh how convenient. i spit but i don't say anything as i have at least fifty years of trading with armani left before i die. "no," she says, "this is not swimwear, this is underwear." like a demonic loony i tell her about the covent garden tube poster with the word 'swimwear'.

she shrugs her shoulders. i cannot hide my disappointment, make my excuses and leave. i've had it up to here with the whole bloody, or should i say fucking, saga, so the following monday i do something i should have done 5 years ago: call up the boss.

"i wish to speak to mr giorgio armani please." "who is speaking sir?" "tell him it is justin cooke." "one moment please sir." the line gives it those satellite cackles and reverbs, there are mutterings and then finally:

"good morning, this is giorgio speaking, what can i do for you justin?" i explain the whole story.

"justin," he says, "i am so sorry for the mix-up. we made a terrible mistake with the posters and i apologise with all my heart for the terrible attitude of my staff. please, i beg you, come out to my villa. i will create a couture pair of white trunks just for you." and that is how i became the first boy in the world (i later found out that johnny w actually wore white pants, hemmed up by his aunt) to have a pair of real, white, swimming trunks.

the st⬤ne

Text & Image   Ralph Wepham

I found a stone on the beach by the sea. I found a stone that could see. I am eight years old and naked. Pulling off cold, damp swimming trunks, crouching to grab my towel and there it is. Staring with its one crocodile eye. Staring at the sky. Then at me.

Cold, dry, smooth, it fitted snugly in my hand. I took it and showed it the world.

I showed it my world. My family. The house where we lived. The car and the hedges. The fields blurring past. I showed it the mysteries of me. I licked it and smiled. Salty smiles. I showed it TV, the caring and suffering there, the world in a box, wonderful pictures that shine. I showed it love, showed it hate, my knuckles and me.

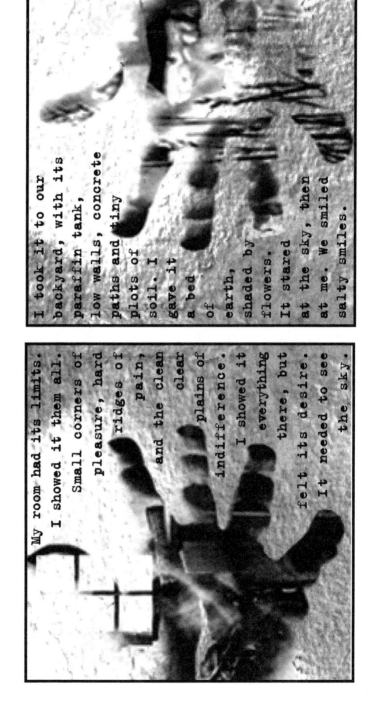

My room had its limits. I showed it them all. Small corners of pleasure, hard ridges of pain, and the clean clear plains of indifference. I showed it everything there, but felt its desire. It needed to see the sky.

I took it to our backyard, with its paraffin tank, low walls, concrete paths and tiny plots of soil. I gave it a bed of earth, shaded by flowers. It stared at the sky, then at me. We smiled salty smiles.

No blame in my
pain. Don't please
misunderstand me.
There was no blame.
A child knows its own
special madness.
That it sees with
different eyes,
inevitably drifting
towards the accepted
world, but still
clinging to the
world it understands
and loves. The world
it has created.
Knowing that one day
it has to let go.

Home from school one day,
milk and biscuits. Out to
kick ball to wall. New
wall. Topped with beach
stones. My dad's deft
hands. Sand, cement and
bricks. Decorative
topping. I knew it was
gone. I scoured the top
of the new wall seeking
the inevitable. Buried
there in concrete. The
worst pain of all, its
eye down, its back to
me. Blinded, never to
stare at the sky again.
We cried salty tears.

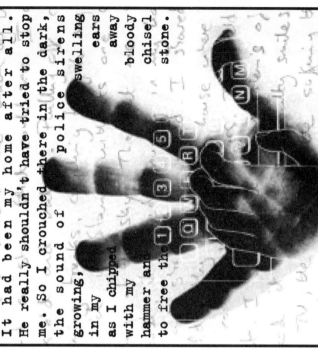

I told them the whole story, how I grazed my elbows and knees getting over the wall of the old home into the back yard. How the tools clanked in the bag. Of course it was the noise. I told them that I was sorry about that man.

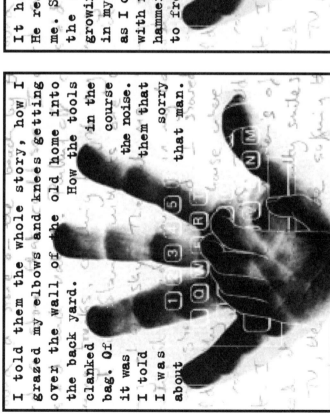

It had been my home after all. He really shouldn't have tried to stop me. So I crouched there in the dark, the sound of police sirens growing, swelling in my ears as I chipped away with my bloody hammer and chisel to free the stone.

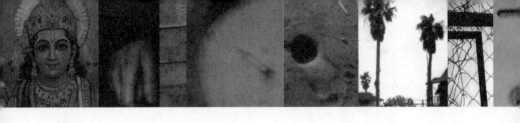

"7

8

9

10"
He was counting her into the sea of her subconscious. "How we doin'?"
Silence.
"Good," he continued. "Now fink in your mind, back to your childhood. When I come to the age where you feel somefink happened I want you to raise your hand. All right?"
Alex grunted. "OK then."

"10

9

8

7"
Alex felt she wasn't really hypnotised. This was partly because of the man's aggravating accent, and partly because her mind was not on her childhood but with Bronwyn, the giant nanny. It was becoming increasingly clear that there was more going on inside Bronwyn than her oafish exterior suggested, particularly when it came to the subject of Alex herself. *The bitch is watching me.*

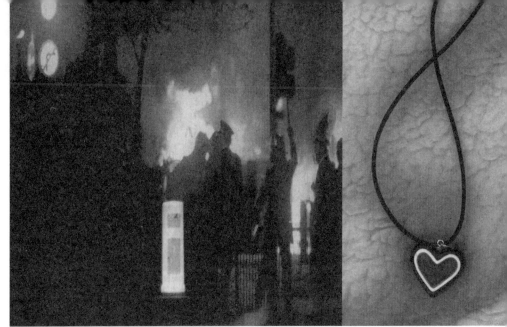

From, 'Still', a novel in progress by

Julia Brosnan

The House of Chains

She knows. That morning Alex was manically hiding the night's dirty evidence before the children got up, when she turned and saw her—Bronwyn bold in piped flannel pyjamas and fat staring eyes, giving off a definite air that if someone ought to explain or apologise it certainly wasn't her.

"6   5   4"

Alex raised her thin hand briefly. She felt it hover upward and took the ride, letting it go. Maybe 4 was significant, or maybe her brain had randomly flickered and jerked her bones into a twitch. Who knows? *I'm paying him. He's supposed to be curing me, let him sort it out.*

"And what can you remember, in your mind, at that time? 4 years old. 4 years old."

Alex was silent. A small, dark haired nervy person with a habit of wrapping her limbs round furniture, her legs were currently clamped up the chair. He tried to coax her. She was irritated, feeling less hypnotised by the minute. This was his fifth attempt. Each time she went along with his counting and chanting and even floated off for the odd second, but it was turning out like all her other half-tried, half-cocked treatments. She always began with tremendous hope, feverishly wanting to believe. But the truth was that she was now as stone cold awake and alert as someone in a permanent state of exhaustion could be. Especially a woman with an expanding husband, 2 unpleasant children and a job that sucked her dry as a prune. Especially on a hot afternoon in a sofa.

"4 years old," he said again. "Hold on, in your mind. Imagine a day. What?"

For an instant Alex was transported by the feel of something cold and heavy on her cheek, something solid and reassuring. *My splintered mind is drawn together.*

"What?" he repeated.

"Pardon?" she said, raising her hand to her face. Her cheek was bare.

"What is the day? What day is it?"

Suddenly back with him, she felt a swell of anger. *That does it. He must know I'm not hypnotised. No one in a trance says pardon.* She wanted to ask him what his qualifications were, whether he was registered with the British Board of Hypnotherapists, but knew she should have done it at the start. Besides, part of her wanted to hang onto the notion that she was a 30 year old adult person, zipped into polished work suits, topped off with a cool folli-plus perm. Women of status and responsibility don't get taken in. She was also desperate. Clinging to the remains of her first brave hope—still a small chance that one day it might work. But he wasn't making it easy.

"Fink about it, fink about it," he sang with airy confidence and through half closed eyes she saw that he was reading the words out of a book on his lap. Alex sighed. It wasn't so much that he was a charlatan but the fact that he was so incredibly bad at it. Wearily she leaned back and was stung, literally stung, by a sharp metallic taste invading her mouth. She gasped as a hot molten steam rose to her nose.

"Back we come," he was saying. "3   2   1...

...And when I snap my fingers..." He snapped them. "There. How d'you feel?"

Alex stared at him. Her head was resting in a cloud of gently cooling steel. She felt relaxed.

"I saw you was really gone, and on the number 4. First you was—" He held out his fist to demonstrate. "And then you was—" He drew in a deep theatrical breath.

"That's good," he continued. "Very good, very good. For this week." He smiled and waited expectantly. Alex continued to stare, then blinked a few times to break the spell. Had he really convinced himself he could do it? Mechanically she went for her handbag. *£45 for three quarters of an hour. £1 a minute!* She made a point of paying him in cash. Writing out a cheque or handing over her credit card wouldn't have the same impact. She wanted to get a physical hold on the enormity of the injustice. Peel it out fiver by fiver, personally say goodbye to each note. But this time the impact was skewed: the metal thing had travelled down and was resting on her shoulders. *Nice and snug. Like a helmet.*

"Same time next week?" he said, tucking the booty into his chest.

"Same time next week," said Alex. *Same time next week!* And she was gone.

SHE MADE HER WAY DOWNSTAIRS. It was a large building in Kensington, lots of ladies on the edge of time getting fleeced by unctuous young men, lots of steel and glass. He rented a room for her visits and claimed he saw other 'patients' at his private consulting chamber. The thought of this usually engendered a fulsome snort from Alex, but now she was cold. The helmet was lifting, she was exposed. Through the wide shiny windows she saw people outside melting in the heat, but she was cased in a light chill. Like prepacked cheese. Something was missing, perhaps she was losing her clothes.

The steel and glass followed her into the toilet. Very bright and harsh, so much so that when she looked in the mirror to check if she was still there, she got a shock. The strip lighting and stark surroundings together created such a brutal environment she hardly recognised her own reflection. Her eyes disappeared behind her glasses, her forehead expanded, her cheeks sagged and her executive perm fell limp and wispy. A flaccid, colourless face stared back and she had the look of someone famous. After a bit of scrutiny she came up with the name: *Salman Rushdie*. Great writer, but not a man she wanted to be mistaken for. The image depressed her. She went into a cubicle and sat.

Feeling entirely vacant, Alex managed a vague background awareness of the irony of being behind a door marked 'engaged'. *Please help me.* She hoistered her focus round to the hypnotherapist. Although she'd developed a jokey cynicism towards him, that's where her hopes were. He was it. Without him it was down to her. Things could shift, move apart. *Mind the gap.* Sad hopes slipped to fear. *Who will save me tonight?*

Cold and hunched in this sharp, hostile place she retreated into herself, wrapping her head in her elbows. Scented soapy odour from the basins travelled to her face and banged on her nose to demand entry. Alex rocked back and forth in an attempt to fool it. *Keep calm and it will fade.*

B A N G

Suddenly a knife springs out of her throat and clamps down like a thick steel door at the back of her mouth. Alex chokes. The force is so great it leaps her up. The odd, metallic taste floods her mouth again. A reassuring sensation seeps out down her tubes and round her innards, spreading warm safety. *Nice, nice, much better.*

Invigorated and back in front of the mirror it was easy. She relocated her eyes, brushed her cheeks with powdered lycra and pumped some life into her hair. She opened her mouth wide up close to her reflection. No steel door to be seen. Strange, because she could feel it, firm and solid, sending out bright, calming juices. Yes. It was nearly 2, and hope was returning by the second. A growing excitement crept up her legs at the thought. Sexual, like buying something expensive and reckless. Even more if she was shop lifting. *I'm not going back to work today. I'm bunking off.* As the idea grew, an image of the office afternoon she'd planned came to mind. No meetings, nothing she couldn't do tomorrow. Exhilarated, she went down to the lobby phone and spun Miss Nancy, the young PA, a line about staging something impromptu in a hotel. Alex was impressed by the girl's gullibility, although mildly concerned that it might one day lead her into becoming a Mormon.

Released, she walked out of the building and left the hypno-thing behind.

Striding purposefully along, she led her tongue around her mouth to search out the taste. It was clean and dreamy, a soothing essence from a past time she couldn't quite place. Definitely nothing to do with the hypno-man, definitely way before him. It welled from inside, from a place of deep connection. *Coming home.* At the tube she knew she was arriving. You can always rely on the tube to take you somewhere, any train will do. The lift doors opened with a hearty crunch. A thick, dimensioned sound, loudly bordered with a tinny resonance. It reached into her bones and set her body racing, pumping round, ringing in her ears. It was coming together, her and it, Alex could feel it, like The Beatles. *We can work it out.*

Leaning back on the cheap, prickly train seat she noticed she was travelling away from home. Of course. Going there was almost worse than going back to work. Daytime weekdays did not belong to her. Bronwyn filled the house, scooping up children, droning away to nursery rhyme tapes, coming back from shopping covered in thick clothes and heavy bags. The kids loved her. *Bizarre.* Shaun would be there too, he'd emerge from his study at intervals, looking important in a silk smoking jacket to shout about deadlines, while he drank ever smaller cups of coffee. *He and Bronwyn are eating against the clock, racing each other into enormity.* Alex noticed that as he got bigger so his hot beverages got smaller. And stronger, like tar. She'd be an intruder if she went back now. *Back to the fat people.* She'd have to bite her tongue and join in. *They know.* You can't sleep in the same bed with someone and not notice when they *...spend their nights raging and roaming in a terror.* You can't live in the same house and not wonder about the mess in the morning.

Walking up the station stairs, holding the rail, sliding the flesh of her hand along the smooth, worn metal surface she remembers. *When the hard steel links first clipped around my skin and the snap of the lock hit like an injection of pure joy.* This is it. She is off to make a purchase.

ALEX VAGUELY KNEW THE AREA and started up the High Street. She guessed she was looking for a cycle shop but was open to persuasion. She took a turning into the Arndale Centre. After walking a few minutes along mall-ways looking for hints as to where she (and a relevant shop) might be, she became aware of how stifling it was. Glaring artificial lights beat down on shoppers already uncomfortable from the heat on the street. The grey skins of people who worked there were parched from the dry bright air, as they toiled away with no breeze or sunshine to wash out their pores. As she walked on, each turning opened up a whole new walkway of ever more garish shopfronts and she was amazed at the size of it. Acres more shops had no fronts at all, spilling themselves out into the eyes and arms of passers by, so it was unclear what was shop and what wasn't. Alex saw a girl selling sunglasses, quite posh ones, on an open stall. She darted about like a mother bird, neck jerking furiously, up and down from goods to customer vainly trying to keep a handle on the stock. The open plan nature of the outlets was an easy invitation to the vacant youths who slouched round the fountains, bored and dangerous. Alex saw it in the pinched features of the sales staff, eyes scanning, joints stiffened, awaiting the inevitable. The tension seemed to be trapped in the building, swallowing away the air. She sensed the oxygen being hoovered up into the enormous glass dome at the top. She was finding it hard to breathe.

Alex turned yet another corner and found herself in a market. The shopping centre was under one vast roof, yet sections of it clearly pretended they were out of doors. The market ladies were wrapped in large cardigans and boots. The men wore caps and cupped their hands around steaming polystyrene beakers. A little farther on a self-styled continental cafe boasted frothy cappuccinos on pavement tables. Several people sat wiping milky moustaches away, rolling up their sleeves and leaning back to enjoy the sunshine. Alex went stiff. Everyone else seemed to understand the place. Passers by were completely unconcerned by its size, unfazed by its content. They knew where shops ended, they knew when they were indoors, they even seemed to know where they were going. Something was banging inside her head like a blacksmith's hammer. *I only want a chain.*

She looked at other shoppers for clues and noticed a strain of remarkably similar young men. Aged about 20, with the bodies of thin 13 year olds. Completely flat and shapeless with concave stomachs and jeans hanging off them like skirts. Cardboard, with a foldaway look, tight strained faces, tiny cotton-top tufts of hair. They were wizened figures, half boy half old man. They walked beside even smaller girls, younger than them in tiny skirts and cheap sleeveless tops. Weary with effort, their pale thin arms stretched forward, manoeuvring enormous pushchairs that dwarfed them. From the back, their spindly legs bowed out with each tired stride. From the front, lumpen babies lay collapsed, dazed in a stupor of fizzy drinks and frosted pop tarts.

Alex's vision was clouded. So many were passing by so often, they could have been on a loop. *Hold on to it. The lock will turn so that something in the back of my head shuts down. Like a computer, leaving me free to dream.* Through the mist an obese woman listlessly sat and gazed at a burger as a great purple girl banged her head, backwards and forwards into the handle of a nearby pram. Rhythmically the woman slapped her, creating a percussion in human bones. She had the same eyes as the tiny gaunt couples, dead in their sockets. Alex felt a great blast of sadness rise up and assault her stomach. She stared at the girl. She was about 4 years old. *4 years old.* A massive blast of hot air billowed into her face, a burning liquid stink of heat welded aluminium. The girl let out a wail and Alex ran.

She seemed to have hit the rough side of town. *Shaun can lock me up at nights and keep me safe.* She slowed down and reminded herself it was only a shopping centre, but it felt like Harlem. A young man was shaking and vomiting in a doorway. She stepped into a pool of violet muck. *It's raining, I'll get soaked.* Shaun did it when they first got married, wanting to help and be sympathetic. Then he got nervous in case there was a fire and she couldn't get out. *Doesn't he know I'd rather burn to death?* Really he was nervous because it was weird. *I can't chain you up any more Alex, I really can't.* This time he'll have to, it's so much worse. *I can't be left to roam around, I'm not responsible.* I'll tell him it's for his own protection. This time I'll save *him* from a burning. *Do it or I'll set you on fire.*

IT IS RAINING HARDER NOW. Alex looks for shelter but all the shops are boarded up. The girl is long gone but her wails still buzz. Several people walk past nervously, staring, and through her damp hair Alex sees that they are dry and crisp. It isn't raining. *It was me. I evaporated.* It's only a shopping centre, thinks Alex. There isn't any weather. Only a shopping centre. The thick cold sweat causes her to shake. *I had to get out.* She belts forward, stiff wet legs sliding across the rubbery floor, and there is a chink of light. Real light and full bodied air. She hauls open the door and flings herself outside, where she crouches wet and gasping on the pavement. When she lifts her head she sees a dim glassfronted shop opposite. She can't distinguish the bulky outlines within, but the sign above catches her eye: **The House of Chains**. She has arrived.

r u s h

a long way from H

Caroline Bergvall

SO where do you come from. We're in the interior, the innermost, the farthest in, the last bar, the inner country, beyond the beating heart, at the quiet core of the jungle riot. The two standing in front of me carry a certain air of, they have an air of, a look about them. YEAH? WHERES that. Subsound long hands sofa pulsations. So WHATS your name & we who filtered who come through. I wonder whether I look kindajazz or excitingly passée. The one to my lefts got studs all over her face like stick-ons & we who seek to inhabit our contours. Well, my grandmother was not a fisherwoman but my family lived

[here]

so as a child I spent years WHAT WAS THAT WHAT WAS THAT avoiding stepping on the algae are gluey and disgusting how they twine around your legs OH how dyou spell that OH with a v for bulge & we who travel small distances all the time and at all times.

Now we're walking a long corridor, down a set of stairs

through soundproof double-doors to some kind of main area the aquarium the tranceball the sheer volume in here pushes a) your hair back b) your eyeballs forward with loud silent laughter. SO whatre you doing here, she shouts. I trip over a block of solid space and nod indifferently, the floor is gigantic, leaves a coloured trail when I blink and flashes up intermittently across this human wave would make for very poor landscapes but to be in it: in-it : gives a wonderful stretch to the body. And grounds the eye-frame somehow.

Listen (says I), I dont mean to be rude but. The one to my right is wearing a beady charm dangles loosely between her breasts are pressed down in a tight stripy blue T-shirt gives her a Querelled sort of a feel. WELL? We've pushed some other doors, we're sinking in low armchairs along dark walls (strange place), the searching flicker of gazes hits the skin which in turn absorbs the heat or throws it back according to some wonderful little pheronome activity which

29

recognizes your taste without you having to take part at
this stage. Do you LIKE it here. Well, backyards sub-
streets roadmarkings maps within maps, Ive been

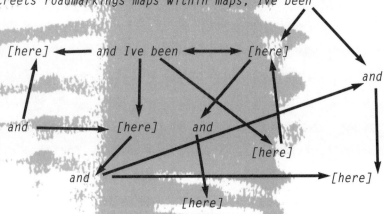

but (the clothes the sound the speak the feel the sex)
whatever might get me closer to H, I havent been [here] I
mean really here yet & we who come through only partially
Im keen to try.
—TELL me (to Querelle) ARE YOU sure that what you think
you show is who I think you are, I ask in a roundabout
(take-me) sort of a (youre-so-cool) way.
The digital imagings floating on the inner walls are
dubbing our conversation and papering the eye :Field.
   Says she who looks startled and hands me a drink:
—Better believe it. Here HAVE A whiff of this.
   Plastic flowers bubble up on my table. Nothing new under
the: belt but how it.
—Come on youre on logged in connected LETS start,
interrupts the other one. Shes a restless sort of a fella,
given to public displays in her clumpy kind of shoes and
her clumpy kinda walk, "its a feat its a gas its a lip its

a beard, arsehole, its my spot stranger, it could be yours for a fiver at the entrance and a rub-in as you go. BUT are YOU one of us." She is shaking my arm, are you, what, one of US.

OH (behaviour known as strap-and-come), "interesting", me thinks, "identities circulate en masse, grow in numbers, slowly, through the obligatory dreams, through the famille, then through ones chosen spot, this is done this isnt, this we worship this we dont, from walk to walk, and bar to bar, we fall to peak, some died for this, forevermore specifying ourselves locally, conceptually to one another: more or less assimilating which field we want to be a part of , which we already are (a part of), breaking these down into smaller and smaller units of behaviour, This rule affects That humour: This wear brings on That carriage: This visibility or That impasse: That possibility or This dead-end, the way These roads get closed to traffic, makes it difficult to keep track of oneself let alone decipher others homecodes & we who need to push through and gather up by the hundred thousands.

AM I one of us, hmm (thinking, drowning in a large pitcher, swimming in an ashtray) & we who need to accumulate all manners of conduct bearing demeanour gathering up details (shsh hairdo my forane accent) the momentum to identify: to wish to be: to belong: identified-identifiable, are you one, I am, one of us, I am, who are you one of those, I am.

Theyre leading me on: I will follow to where this goes,

shaking off a persistent flicker, boldly on our way we go
to play out a shared sense of us, what it is that brought
us here. Hm, wondering whether us will require props of any
kind. And also: (why me) I really have very little gear, my
bag, my shoes, thats about it, no facial femhair no
discernible grit so I dont know are you looking for a
fully-styled cued-up sort of a tendency, a vague
inclination or just a good time in a friendly environment.
—Why, dont you KNOW where you are.

Oh doors open Oh they close And I walk in through the
gap. Whatever gets me closer to. Perhaps Ive missed the
cues. I know that attitudes are often sketchy and therefore
difficult to keep. Just talking to you could give me a bad
name if your particular type was running out of favour. But
a bad reputation is nothing like a bad attitude. A bad
attitude can give you a good reputation. Now thats good for
business. But a bad reputation is never good for business,
in fact is only ever BAD for business. And whats bad for
business is bad for us (not you: me, my group, my patch but
we are expanding so if you ever need ...:..:: or
::......";..... heres my card). Listen, EUH, (anyway). Sure
I do sure I DO. But am I one, one of us (of us of us of
us). And whose big close-up is this peering into my left
eye anyway.

By now we're all getting fairly ::::: :::: ::. and a
long way from H. Faces: are reaching me wide angle: red
mouths pressed into my long vue view. HEY! Thats her thats
her! I tell them breathlessly having just seen you parading

your stuff for a group of tourists. Never told me you were

Egyptian. She says, Gaps grow like   missing   houses:

Speed: this specific zone in space and time. Theres a

constant flicker flashing in my eyes. Its not that I wish

to (please tick):

☐   cut corners
☐   interrupt the manner of our exchanges
☐   burn bridges
☐   rush your beard
☐   forget forget
☐   other (specify)...

but could we get back to the point (say I). HAH! both

exclaiming HAH in unison. I mean am I kindajazz HAHAH or

just passée (cant BELIEVE I just said DID I just say that,

that) & we who always look for new locations I always seem

to get my hand (stuck too) stuck too deep into the throat

of some:: other travel   ling:: mutants:: close closer the

closest to H, how we end up:: glued to each other,

siamesed, last time I had to be cut loose: hacked: axed

away HAH HAH DYOU want a drink or somethi***

theyre   here ::: breathe in   theyre here: : breathe

out: theyre ::::   gone: someone : ::: this

reverb this   wind: to hear: to hear: :   waw — a waw—

a   the sea   is dark-er   : :   where   the

coastline is   smooth slides   into   the water

shes   holding   me by   the   hand   to get   the

crabs   outof   the net: ::   whos got white   hair

tied   back   and whistles   then shes   gon***

Theyre grabbing me by the shoulders, dragging carrying

me out, down the stairs, long the corridor, forcing water

over my face, between my lips, is this happening to me, yes
yes yes yes ye*** :   :   the house   behind :::: me
its white-painted   wood catches :. fire can see
a face right up   to :mine   who is it   repeat repeat
repeat   re   peat   the   bloodline   drags   one
fin ger on the   map then   m   lost   Im los t h e
trees   ar   tall   an   tight   behin d   me
:   closing in   on   m :: push   e   ou t
"give bread to the floreigner!" th   towncrier   brea t
hing   dow   n   my   ne k   who ties
y : : : tong ue in o   three   soli   d
knot s   throws   me   ou   of   to wn   a t   the
last strok   of   midnigh***

  THEYre carrying me towards the exit, make way, check my
pupils, WHATS your name WHERE dyou come from, this is the
time, youll be OK, when spasmodic bodies are recovered from
the corners, under the tables, behind the chairs & we who
would mostly like to sleep in our own beds of this gigantic
submarined trancehall.

WAILING WALL

Jacqui Palmer

I was at the wailing wall
But I wasn't wailing
I was at the dead sea floating
I was eating cake and icecream and
watermelon
with my girlfriends
I was hanging on for dear life
Went to movies
and the beach
Took some pictures
bad ones
Tried to tell them
Couldn't
Took my knickers off on the beach
Just for the sheer hell of it
And the wrangle with the lifeguard
No secrets in here I said
But he didn't catch it
In Hebrew or English
Sat in cafes
smoking cigarettes
Walked around the market buying turkish
coffee and nuts
Thought I'd bring it all back
To my little room
That place
Pulled her arm told her I was mourning
Scared
Alone
Can I have him back I asked her
Called him
No reply
Could float in the dead sea
Eternally maybe
If it didn't sting my bum

FREEDOM CITY

Michael Onile-Ere

Time out at the mobile. Another pit stop. All fully oxygenated. Chris taking refreshment orders and luring a jazz poet back to the car who's going our way. He has a bag of pills stashed in an artificial scrotum that he pulls out without turning blue.

"I am Django," he says, while settling his rump between myself and Mitch. "Madames, sirs, allow me to read some of my jazz poetry before we delve."

Everyone's loving his outlandish behaviour, his larger than life parody. I am Django: no inquisitive banter, no brief life history, just dandy flamboyance. Everything about him says woman, except that you know he will slit your warm throat or split your cold nose if you go for his scrotum…A real live wire drama queen!

"Okay boys and girls listen up, stop talking, Django doesn't like it." And he is clapping his hands like a gym instructor in gold legwarmers and matching headband.

"Okay this is it," he says clearing his throat for the fifth time, until we are all hush hush:

Django random cat sits on a snazzy pouffe drinking tea from a large urn and clicking fours to a frantic jazz bop beat.
Joe blows a long thin pipe, rolls his eyes and sees the sky turn yellow.
Django purrs and issues smoky vibrations,
now the room is yellow, but Joe swears it always was and blows some more.
Speak loose, then tight, fast slow blow man blow,
This time it's a neat in time number played to a bassy drum roll and snatches of percussion from icy symbols.
Crush Sizzle!
Spy a sweat soaked shirt and watch it melt off his groovy forehead then wash his face.
Under all that yellow sky, and out comes blue notes, and now it's hip,
See it!
Makes mad faces and flirts with his bopping jazz heads.
Likes to give them the big tease.
Crash! now falling off with eyes so slitty he's squeezed the vision out of them.
Joe blows, his wrist veins pulse in time,
And when he howls wolf cries the whole room pushes out air from ballooning guts,
And a girl in a rain mac opens her mouth and swallows the sound.

"I like that," says Chris.
"Yeah," I say, "it's cool like jazz," and I try to make the sound that comes out of a sax, and imagine the words floating on the notes, riding it like a musical wave.
"How are you young lady, and why are you travelling with such riff raff?" says Django.

Kim smiles. "Django's a nice name," she says. "Thank you darling, I'll remember you when it comes to serving time…Right, don't disturb me," he says. …And with that he drops off to sleep for half an hour. Only he's not really asleep, just sussing us out. When he opens his eyes again he tells us he's decided to come clean. Django's revealing that he's not a jazz poet at all, that he found the piece in a bop magazine.

"It's an act. In my line of work, trust is a commodity you can't afford, but you children look safe."

"So this is the reward we get for picking you up," says Chris. And Django starts telling us how easy it is for paranoia to take a firm grip on your shoulders and pull you down, so that one day you wake up and think that your own brother, flesh and blood, could be a narcotics agent.

"A plant from your mother's womb, so to speak…but in you kids I recognise a breed." Now he's saying, "anything you want I can get."

But we don't know enough names, so we sit there getting high on some weed and are willingly coaxed into swallowing anything he recommends. Mitch has an amusing habit of scrutinising everything he is given as if looking for flaws in the chalky button consistency. Kim doesn't even look, treats it like she's got migraine and is dropping aspirin. I say my prayers and try to forget that something weird is dissolving about my insides…Then I tell myself that this is it, you're up… then I think no this isn't it…then I spend twenty minutes trying to decide whether this is a placebo or not…Chris holds his pill up to the light and tries nibbling. Then he decides to crunch! and

ends up with a face like a prune, complaining how disgusting it tastes. And Django, he treats them with indifference, taking two at a time for the hell of it.

The smug grins are taking over…Here's Mitch, his crooked face gradually drifting off-centre, like the left side and the right are fighting over facial territory…They arrive at a truce…till the left tries to swap positions and starts slowly creeping around whenever the right's not looking but has to stop when his nose won't budge……And Kim's hair hangs there minus Kim…just a shiny blonde wig suspended in mid-air…Now that's me, Max, bending forward to make sure that her head and body have not melted away…There they are… And that dress so tight it's breathing…its folds and creases breathe like gills…and what about that special force field around her body, drawing in male eyes…and inside that, the even stronger one that burns and stings the iris if you exceed reasonable gazing time.

The inside of the car is glowing. We are sitting in the middle of a white light but it doesn't dazzle. All hard surfaces soften to a rubbery goo with no perspective, like a very cheap 3D hologram. No texture, no hardline definition, just fuzzy frames and cartoon cushions…Freaky-deaky 3D luminous paint show …All wow and day-glow. And along the front the back and the sides the windows are cellophane peepshows, an outdoor TV network link up. So the movie is rolling…Sound check…Brm! Brm!…It's a wrap…Brought to you by the celluloid live playback soft focus lenswear team…There are no starlets, luvvies or primadonnas in this bratpack, just a fantastically awesome cut. Cut! Beam me up to the stratosphere live at six…What a show we have for the dope heads!

"Yes! Hello everyone, fancy meeting you here!" being the general

thought at this moment.

Django is feeding us more pills and the smiles are getting bigger…Pill number three, and Chris suggests that we stop… "And you wouldn't mind going for a stroll in your bubble masks while Kim and I get rid of some of this sex tension would you?"

"What, here, now?" says Mitch.

"I don't like to ask, but…" says Chris.

"Come on guys, Chris has got the horn," says Mitch.

But Kim says that her period is due any second, and Chris nods back like she told him the whole platoon went down in friendly fire.

Somehow the rest of us get it into our heads that Kim secretly intends to hook up with one of us. We go mad trying to laugh it out of our minds before the unsaid thing is telepathically read by Chris. It's para para para all round the inside of the car, and we're gritting our teeth so we won't suck too much in. Django tries to break the para chain.

"This cat I know once showed me how to lose money at the fair without even trying…There were these cones on a ledge, nailed down like cement bollards I bet. He's supposed to shoot 'em off with a silver pistol that fires rubber darts. He was a big chap, six-four. He leaned forward like a darts expert, and began waving the pistol about shooting in any direction he liked, with absolutely no regard for accuracy. The elderly attendant looked on like he's crazy…"

And now I'm thinking this is a story about Chris and beginning to doubt every wild thing he's ever done. Next to me, Mitch is becoming a cute teenager and confessing his life: "As a kid, I wanted to love every pretty girl I ever met, but I didn't know how, at least I thought I didn't. Only now I realise that you can say love like you say like and vice versa."

"Yeah???" says Kim. "That's holy beautiful. He's a saint ain't he!"

Our driver is wrapped in his own world, he's fixed on ahead like he's looking into next week.

"Alright, Chris," I say.

"Yeah mate," says Chris.

"Hey Chris, are you alright to drive," says Kim.

"You sure that this is the right way," says Mitch.

"Hey Chris, lend us your shades… Hey Chris, how about pulling over for a sec?…Hey Chris, what time is it?… Hey Chris, lend us some credits." Until he says we are milking him dry. He gets all croaked up when he says it: "What d'you people want from me!" And he's proposing to sit in the back and if he hasn't said parasites yet, you know that it's on the edge of his tongue.

Django offers to drive, and panic runs through the car like a bolt of electric. We're not sure why, but we think Chris deserting his post might be a bad omen.[1]

We pull into a side road while Django takes the driver's seat and Chris gets in the back. Django's going on about a short cut. Short cut! He doesn't even know our destination. This could get weird. But nobody argues, he's the driver now…It's no longer the smooth roller coaster ride. Django's saying something about old cars being no good and he's managed to kangaroo twice.

Soon everyone's hating everyone else for some pathetic reason. Kim leans forward to get something out of the glove compartment, and we all take this to mean that she and Django are going well beyond the bounds of mere friendship…Then Chris ignores her and none of us says a single word until Mitch says he feels ill and can he sit in the

---

1 Dr Weed: a brief discussion on drug superstition:
The drug world is highly sensitive to omens. There are layers and layers of hidden meaning, more than an Eng. Lit. student could dream of. We are talking semantics in perverse distress. Pretty soon you're opening the floodgates to a cranium load of the most profound cause and effect imagin-able. Wow! shot right through the subconscious in an explosion of colour-aided knowledge. We have the Key! Now I see the universe unfettered by the constraints of my egotism. Now I realise what it is I am afraid of—the latter turning out to be a bit of a bummer.

front away from the heat. Then I refuse to let Kim in my side of the door, so she has no choice but to curl up next to Chris. It's probably hilarious if you're not in the sketch, an impartial observer. Picture yourself surfing the car bonnet, with your own hand-held camera…filming four kids and a pilled up Santa ready to boil. The steam is rising. Through the mist you can make out the tips of fat fingers, prodding maniacally beyond that sheet of rising moisture, and into the chests of the closest moving target. Thump! And now you see legs kicking out.. Adult legs, but apparently wearing the same woolly grey shorts of eighteen years previous. And the same pinafore with custard stains down the front…These juveniles. A face, once an innocent cherub, now pops through the mist all croaked up, bitter hot and twisted, like the three hags in Macbeth. All sadden from too much self pity, and sulking: precocious infants, see! Too much psychotherapy in their schools, and not enough hard licks.

On one level that's exactly how it looks. But if we stop… Time out! Cut!… or better still escape from our bodies, we'd see ourselves from the outside looking in…around aged five, saying, "It's not my fault, *they* started it Miss," as we turn stool pigeon on the whole infant world. But not Django. He eyes the road nervously, because that's the way it is when your fat neck is exposed to four psychopaths.

Now we are all hassling for elbow room. Jab. jab. jab…Ouch! The car must be shrinking. Maybe the car is shrinking! and forcing us into this tight-tight squeeze…The human gridlock. Like everyone's far too close for comfort man. When one farts all feel it. We are talking Baaad Vibrations! The heat's rising. All those hearts going thwack thwack thwack! Sounding off like a million and one scrambled beats. Thwack thwack thwack the anginal cats choir, revved up to a dangerous sounding maximum. I daren't think of it. I mean which of those ill sounding thwacks is mine?

Mitch wants to get out because he's had just as much as he can take, but Django keeps passing joints, and pushing on faster than ever…Then everyone gets nice swallowing Django's pills again. Somewhere along the line we agree that we're overdoing it, but we're not sure how to stop. We're not even convinced it'd make any difference. Now we're all sorry as hell. Kim says she is buzzing off her nut…I say "Mental mental mental!" and everyone looks at me like I'm the one off my nut. Django's coming back to life, too high on his pills to worry about psychopaths. He's past caring; ready to befriend the most terrifying ogre and tame the hell out of him. He boasting how if he gets pulled by the law he has the ability to shed his skin and reshape as a DS officer.

"Nobody can touch me," he says. "I've got ID cards as well." Which he doesn't show us…

"I'm the original invisible man. You've probably heard of me. Captain Django, buccaneer supreme in the pill serving community, elusive to the point of imperceptibility."

All of us are saying yes yes, because he's giving us pills and we like him. Maybe he is a cop, who cares for now. So we smile, forgive ourselves and forgive each other…There aren't enough hours in a day to waste whingeing. We've got a buzz to uphold!

My head rattles so much that everywhere I look the vision stutters… Wow! I love it and I love you all… No more misery, just out of it…Break the chain… Downer …break the chain………… Joy…Pleasure… Ecstasy… Rainbow prisms… Soft cartoon skin. Glow… fire…calm…Coming down nicely…ME/YOU all the same one, one mind troupe, one will… One tribe………Everything a plastic dream toytown, and I love it.

Billy England's
BOOK OF PAIN

Extract from *Billy and Girl*, a new novel by Deborah Levy

Soon all the kids in England will be pushing up daisies.

That's what Girl says every night before I go to sleep. Girl is my sister and I'm scared of her. She's seventeen years old, got ice in her veins and tonight she reads me my rights. "Billy," she says in that voice like turps, "you have the right to complain about the weather. You have the right to promote Billy products when you're famous. You have the right to help me find Mom and you have the right to tell me what happened to Dad. Which one is it to be?"

Yesterday she bought me a present. A pair of stacked red trainers wrapped in folds of white tissue paper. She likes me to look like a baby gangster and I don't mind, but now I have to pay for them. My sister pretends to be retarded sometimes so she doesn't have to speak or react like other people do. Just as you think she is in Neverland, she suddenly springs on you with her white trash fists.

Girl was in love once. She was nice to me then and bought me a badminton set for us to play in the park. Love made her high enough to sing and jump and swipe the shuttlecock back to me with the toy racket. Her sweetheart was called Prince. He bought me a water pistol and I shot myself in the ear, up the nostrils, in my heart, on the inside of my thigh, dying for the neighbourhood cats with their spacey eyes.

"Which one are you going to choose Billy?" Girl's black eyes, always vacant, conveniently give the impression she is brain damaged.

I am in the womb of my mother who will later disappear without trace. "Don't cry," Girl chides me, twisting her thin lips.

I am in the womb of my mother. I hear car alarms go off and sometimes I hear my father. He says "Hello Babykins. This is your Daddy speaking. We are looking forward to meeting you, over and out." I hear cats purring and Girl shouting, "You're late brother.

Come on out!" I don't want to be born. I'm never coming out. Dad tries again: "Hello Babykins, it's your Daddy here. Time to face the world like a man—look forward to meeting you son. Over and out."

Mom used to stroke my head, babying me. I'd like to eat something with onions in. Pizza or soup. Like Mom used to make before she disappeared. The night before she had me, she swam in shorty pyjamas and ate cinnamon buns.

Life could have been amazing. We could have gone together to the video shop and bought ice cream, jelly beans and micro popping corn. We could have sat at home and watched a film, sprawled on the floor, stuffing ourselves.

Girl says, "No Billy, that is someone else's memory. We never went to a video shop."

Yes we did. When Robocop says "stay out of trouble," I listen to him, but the trouble is in my head. It's in my chest and the back of my neck. After I was born I howled the hospital down. I howled like the heart that had taken nine months to grow would splatter onto the silver stainless steel tray the midwife was holding nearby just in case.

I can see myself clearly as I was then. This is how I came to be Brother Billy in the English climate. I started life as a cell. The male and female chromosomes are fusing. I am two cells. Now I am a cluster of cells. Suddenly I am a tiny embryo embedded in Mom's uterine wall.

Four weeks old and I'm 2mm long. I have the beginnings of a nervous system. No fingernails to chew yet. My hands and feet have ridges which will become fingers and toes. A spinal cord has begun to form. Ten weeks and my kidneys have started to produce urine. I weigh 100g, like a quarter of mince.

By the end of the third month I've grown a forehead, little snub nose and a chin. Watch out family, cuz my lips are beginning to move. I'm never coming out. Even to have a go at them. I'm not going to arrive. I wrinkle my forehead in preparation for sorrow and disgust. I'm learning how to swallow and breathe. Mom is being sick on Dad's best shirt. Afterwards she guzzles salt and vinegar crisps helped by Girl who's always got her sticky white fingers in the bag. Twelve weeks old and I can hear her sharp little teeth crunching crisps. I can hear Mom's heartbeat. I can hear her blood whooshing. Mom is crying and Dad is crying. Girl just snivels. I can hear doors banging.

Eighteen weeks old and I want to retire. That's a long time to live in my book. I've had enough. No such bloody luck. Mom keeps on eating and I keep on growing. I'm sucking my fingers in fucking dread. Oh God. I can taste something. Dad does his regular "Hell-oo Babykins—we're going to call you Bill-ee!" Mom tells Dad to leave the house and never come back. My eyes are tight shut.

I am six months inside Mom

and if I was born now I might survive out of her body. I want a good looking woman lawyer who loves children to take my case to the European courts. I've got toenails. Mom tells Dad I'm pressing against her bladder and she got caught short. Dad laughs and strokes her belly. That's when I open my eyelids and start to kick.

Eight months and my testicles began to descend into the scrotum. I got hiccups. Why? Because Mom's producing adrenalin. It's flooding into the bloodstream. She's frightened. Her fear is leaking hormones into me: I am in biochemical harmony with Mom and I got fear in me too. Now my fingernails have reached the fingertips. I'm going down now, head first. I got a lot of fat laid down ready for the world. Girl is singing something horrible. Mom's got sweet stuff in her breasts waiting for me. Yip, for me. Billeeeee! Thing is I won't be coming out to taste it. Oh no. The weather will be cool out there, I know it. I don't want to arrive.

No No No No Oh God NO!

The midwife pats Mom's forehead with a towel: "He'll give in, don't worry love. He's got the whole family to meet, hasn't he?"

Leave out the formal introductions won't you. I'm sure the family will make themselves known to me in their own good time. All normal infants are supposed to smile aren't they? Laughter is genetically coded into the body. I'm slapping my little white thighs and chortling already.

Dad pulled into a petrol station. He put the pump into his mouth and got five pounds worth. Then he took out his pack of cigarettes and lit up. It was the biggest barbecue South London had ever seen. My father had never smoked before. This was his first and last cigarette and his suicide was the most splendid thing he ever did in his life. Girl and I have talked about it over and over. We decided he must have bought the pack from the newsagent near the Odeon. Coins cold in his hand. Black secret in his heart. Streatham's lone cowboy without horse or bourbon, just an imagination never expressed until now. All the people coming out of the Esso shop clutching sausage rolls and cans of Fanta fell about screaming. A newspaper reporter offered Mom the chance to "open her heart to the world." Afterwards she bought Girl a Sindy doll with long blond hair, a blue bikini, a little pearl necklace and a plastic Ferrari with silver wheels. We set fire to Sindy one night and watched her melt in front of our eyes. Then I went off to watch Loony Tunes outside the TV shop in the mall.

After I was born Mom took special pain killers because they cut her up at the hospital to pull me out. Remember I didn't want to come out. They cut her and then told her to "cross her heels like a cat." Cross your heels like a cat the midwife said, and yanked out the placenta with both hands. I lay on Mom's breast and they stitched her while Dad cried in the corridor, eventually putting his head round the door and whispering "all right pet?"

Why don't they all do something about my "welcome to the world" breakfast? Like a smorgasbord of analgesics and a razor blade?

When Mom took me home she examined my fingernails first. "Look Girl," she said, "they've grown right to the edge and over." So I would scratch my face with my sharp nails. Make little fists and raise them to my cheeks and scratch because it upset Mom and made her kiss me more. She'd sit in a blue bucket under the shower, the smell of lavender she had added to the water filling the steamy corridor where girl and I sat waiting for her. "The lavender fields of Provence, Billy, that's what you can smell," she shouted through the steam, and Girl and I watched the rain splash against windows, shivering in our secondhand tee shirts.

After she had bathed her birth wounds, Mom limped downstairs and made Girl breakfast: banana fritters. Girl wanted banana everything. Banana milkshakes, banana blancmange, banana curry. Mom was a bit nervous of Girl and catered to her compulsions for fear her daughter would weep those catastrophic tears of hers and never stop. When Girl cries the world slows down. It's like her thin white body is going to snap in two because her grief is so total and infinite. In the days we used to go for drives into the country, if she didn't see a horse she'd scream and shout as if somehow this was a bad omen and the sky was going to fall on her head. Dad would get desperate and point to a cow grazing in a field. "There's a horsie Girl, see?" The lie seemed to comfort her, as if just naming the beast completed the magic circle in her ash white head, and she would calm down and fall asleep.

Girl has always invented games for me and her to play together. Her favourite used to be the Bolt game. When she found a jar full of two inch wrought iron bolts in the cupboard under the stairs where all the nails and screws were kept , she showed them to me as if she had found gold in a cave. All day she brooded on what to do with them, hiding behind her fringe of ash white hair when anyone dared speak to her. "It's a pain game Billy," she whispered when Mom went out of the room and the next thing I knew she had dragged me outside and was drawing a chalk line on the pavement which I had to stand behind. Then she measured twenty footsteps away from my line and drew another line which she stood behind. The idea was I had to keep completely still while she aimed the little bolts at my head. When they missed and got me on my shins or on my fingertips I was not allowed to cry. It was a pain game after all, and success was measured by how stoic the person being hit could be. What would it be like to never feel pain?

The day Girl broke the skin on my forehead and blood dripped down my face and onto my tee shirt, she screamed "Don't blink Billy," and then hugged me for being well hard. When I pretended not to feel pain, I know that Girl felt it on my behalf. "You're a hero," she said in her acid drop voice, and licked the warm blood with her tongue while I pretended to meow like a kitten. Girl's pain game prepared me for being bashed by Dad. Girl was training me up to receive pain. It was her way of protecting me. My very own personal pain trainer. The first time Dad smashed his fist into my kidneys I was seven years old.

Mom was out and Girl was in. I hollered and my sister went very quiet. She smoked her first menthol cigarette then. Coughing but no words.

A few weeks after Dad set fire to himself at the petrol station, Mom took me on a coach trip somewhere near Newcastle to meet my grandfather. That's my mother's father. She packed tuna sandwiches and a flask of tea and sat me on her knee in the coach so she wouldn't have to pay for another ticket. I swear I could smell rubber on the tarmac of the motorway and the milk in Mom's breast and when we arrived we heard a fat man in a pub sing England! awake! awake! awake! I lay on her lap under the little tar-

tan blanket and scratched my eyelids, all the time remembering my Dad whispering "Hell-oo Babykins, it's your father here, over and out," scratch scratch and Mom catching my fingers tight in her hands. Grandad talked in whispers to Mom, sometimes leaning over me with his watery eyes and beery breath, checking me out and looking away again, and I swear by the time he gave Mom three green tomatoes grown on his allotment instead of the money I knew she wanted, all of six months old, I thought Jeez, I really need a fag.

"You are my balaclava angel," Girl whispers to me as I hold up the mirror for her while she trims her fringe. No I'm not. I'm a broken hearted bastard.

I want to be the bloke on the Häagen Daz ads, with good looking girls in their underwear pouring ice cream all over my big beautiful body. Instead I'm poor white and stupid. I take my knife into cinemas and stab the velvet seats in the dark. That is my silent broadcast to the British nation.

Pain is like lager and elastoplast. It has made me who I am.

At night I hide in small gardens outside here and count the TV aerials. I click the heels of my new red trainers three times, take a deep breath, hold my nose, and wait for the wind to take me somewhere better than this.

ABOUT LISA a small bad story in 12 good parts. *Tim Etchells*

1

The boss at DAVE'S TOPLESS CHIP SHOP is called Harry Stannington. The shop is just a franchise and the real Dave is more of a marketing proposition than a proper person.

Harry Stannington is a pathetic lying police informant who's going to get his head kicked in and his tongue cut out, at least if you believe the graffiti someone has sprayed outside the shop.

2

Harry fancies a new girl that works in the CHIP SHOP who is called Lisa. Harry keeps asking her out but for at least a month she says no.

Lisa is basically an unlucky misery guts with a hidden gift for brilliant ideas.

Putting her top back on after work one day she finally caves in and agrees to go out with H. Stannington.

4

It's one of those films where the plot is just a flimsy excuse put together to justify a procession of different sentimental conversations—at hospital bedsides, on dusky beaches, in empty offices and at tearful breakfast tables.

That night Lisa's sister gets murdered and Lisa blames herself—if she hadn't gone out it would never have happened etc.

3

Lisa and H. Stannington go to the pictures. They have to walk thru something like a forest to get there. There seem to be cats stuck up in all the trees—yowling madly and miaowing to get down.

When they get to the pictures Harry doesn't like the film but pretends he does. Lisa also doesn't like it but can't be bothered to pretend.

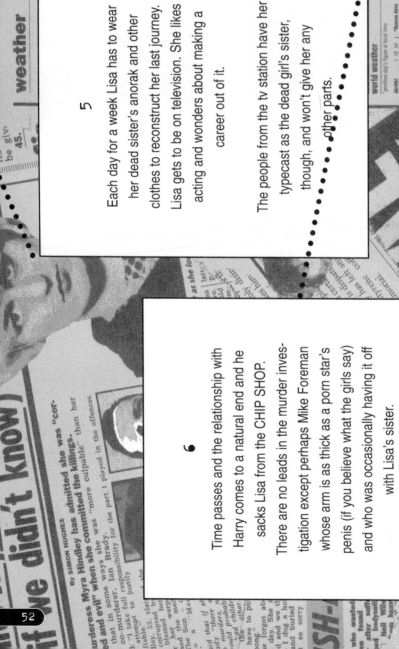

5

Each day for a week Lisa has to wear her dead sister's anorak and other clothes to reconstruct her last journey. Lisa gets to be on television. She likes acting and wonders about making a career out of it.

The people from the tv station have her typecast as the dead girl's sister, though, and won't give her any other parts.

6

Time passes and the relationship with Harry comes to a natural end and he sacks Lisa from the CHIP SHOP. There are no leads in the murder investigation except perhaps Mike Foreman whose arm is as thick as a porn star's penis (if you believe what the girls say) and who was occasionally having it off with Lisa's sister. Mike hangs out in the Bull & Patriot pub—everyone knows he's guilty but there's no evidence.

One day Lisa sees Mike Foreman going down a side alley and knowing that the law is an arsehole and that Forearm is a murderer she kills him dead, with no regret.

The gods (such as they are) are pretty angry abt this and Zeus, Tesco, Venus, Mr Stretchy, Penelope, Kali and all the rest are all having a big row and making various wagers abt what will happen next.

7

Lisa has a dream where she wins the Eurovision Song Contest singing a song in Portuguese. Later in the dream she is back with H. Stannington having sexual intercourse in the TOPLESS CHIP SHOP and he is imploring her:

"Speak Rwandan to me, speak Rwandan, I like it when you speak Rwandan..."

These kind of crazy dreams drive Lisa crazy.

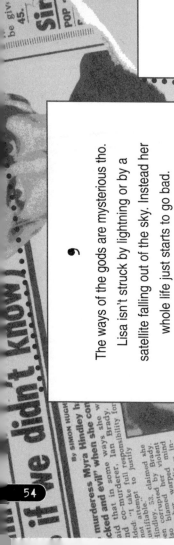

10

Later (probably July) the automatic doors in all the buildings in the city seem to ignore her and no longer open anymore, like they know she is no longer human or worse perhaps no longer a living thing of any kind.

Only by waiting for a stray dog to trigger the infra-red can Lisa get in anywhere.

9

The ways of the gods are mysterious tho. Lisa isn't struck by lightning or by a satellite falling out of the sky. Instead her whole life just starts to go bad.

To start she has panic attacks, and many many long nights of sleeplessness. Her room is burgled (twice times), flooded (also twice times) and burnt a bit in a fire that is something to do with a persistent electrical fault.

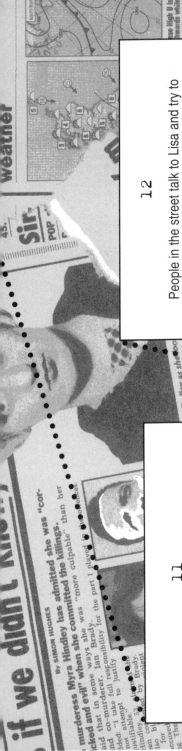

12

People in the street talk to Lisa and try to act like everything is OK, but machines and most animals ignore her.

Lisa changes her name by deed poll. She calls herself something more suited to her age, race, sex and occupation. She calls herself SILENCE. And from that moment on she lives up to her name.

THE END

11

Lisa gets more bad luck. She gets a skin complaint and falls out with her mum. Her new job at The Institute For Physical Research doesn't last.

Before long Lisa can't even see her image on the CCTV screens in town and she knows she's disappearing. She understands quickly that this is the punishment the gods have meted out for her vengeance of her poor innocent sister.

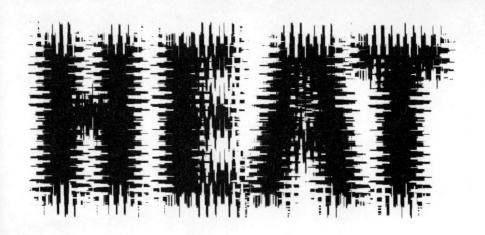

TIM HUTCHINSON

The sound of traffic came like waves, a sea dream
that drove the temperature higher still. The
afternoon was already drifting into evening and the
only way to get through the night was to drink until
he passed out. Too hot to move, he drank vodka out of
a glass with a cow on it, thinking on disconnected
levels. Plague in a desert seemed sexy. A knifing
outside Rome station on a night like this seemed
intellectual. She was sitting at the kitchen table
drinking a glass of water; brown from travelling,
with knotted hair. He listened while she told stories
that made everything better. Rage came in through the
window in car horns and screams.

    He had been at the lido all day watching the
bodies around him turn into leather. Women lay
reading and taking their tops off slowly, trying to
make it seem like they had always been naked. That
act of unclothing fascinated him. It was like a
release, the moment before the breasts came out
tense; shall I shan't I in the air. Afterwards it was
natural and everywhere and the men wished that they
could feel the same. Some boys pointed and jeered at
nipples. Like being at the seaside, the pool was a
little island where wild animals came to drink.
Lifeguard whistles blew intermittently at slight
indiscretions.

    The walk to the bus stop reminded him of walking
along the seafront with sand in his trunks as a

child. The traffic made the temperature hotter and the road a volcanic stream. Yesterday a young man was pulled from the canal, from the same spot where divers had hurled themselves at the water the previous Sunday. The market came to life anyway and a swarm of wasps descended on the fruit. He thought a great deal about water. It was so much a part of his life. He remembered the sea in his dreams, he lived by the river, went to work along the canal. On his days off he went to the pool.

She shared his afternoons and they talked about their week. In the front room they had discussions that went on for ever, perhaps because of all the books in the room. Even if they didn't decide anything, at least they felt good because they'd been talking. In the bedroom things got too close to the bone, it was a mind blow. In the kitchen it could be violent because of the things to grab and threaten with. Things never resolved themselves in the hallway. They were too close to the front door and a way out.

People wore less and less. When the wind blew, the thin fabric of their clothes outlined their muscles; their stomachs and their groins. A car tyre had split in the heat and the small withering bushes in the park floundered. He saw a man changing his clothes in an upstairs room.

Back at the flat they turned on the radio. That afternoon in three different parts of the city there had been three different murders. A small girl abducted, stabbed and left in a field; two boys out fishing had been strangled and a woman on the Docklands Railway kidnapped, raped in the train and left at Mudchute. Weird to connect that with the idea of four thousand dead Serbs.

She cracked open a bottle of beer and it bubbled up onto the kitchen floor. It was easy to imagine how two people could tear each other apart in such weather. He went over to the window. Some teenagers were showing their arses to the passing traffic. There were a vast amount of seagulls. Weird because they were nowhere near the sea. Their scree scree filled each new day with tension and violence as they tore the city apart with their superior beaks.

Her first bottle was already empty. Too hot to eat, they moved to the bedroom which was cooler than the front of the house as the window overlooked the gardens. Someone had turned a sprinkler on; over and over the droplets died into the grass. A man with a glass of wine in one hand was hosing his lawn, the water drenching someone else's washing on the line over the fence. He didn't notice.

They had sex, though they'd had a shower and it meant having another. Sometimes they had sex in the shower, it saved energy. Afterwards he heard the faint high-pitched buzzing of a horsefly that had come in through the window. He remembered it was time he watered the plants. She came out of the shower as he was leaning over the cheese plant. It grew fast in this weather. The room was like a greenhouse. She opened another bottle and turned on the telly. On the news Julia Somerville said how six men had been murdered on the same night in different places by different people in the same city.

"All this violence. Must be the heat," she said, looking at a mark on her leg that hadn't been there in the afternoon.

He pointed at a scratch on his back and smiled.

They watched tv for a couple of hours, wondering whether or not to fuck again.

He woke up. A strange light was coming into the bedroom. Too early for morning, yet he couldn't remember a night this hot. He heard shouting in the alley between the gardens. Sounded like a fight. He couldn't move. It was kind of nice listening to violence. He wondered if he should get up and take a look. He sat up and looked at the moist patch where he'd been sleeping. She was splayed out unconscious. There was a smell of someone smoking a fag in the garden below. Maybe the guy next door couldn't sleep either. He often saw him standing in the middle of the lawn late at night.

He couldn't remember a summer like this. Inside his blood it made him feel ill. He needed water.

Like a new day the room slowly got redder. He moved over to the window. The house next door was on fire.

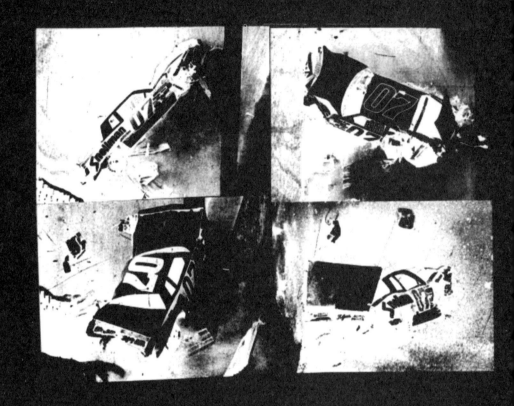

ROOTING

Robyn Conway

A Terrible Journey.

As well as the cow they carried pigs on board, a large number of them,
and these were allowed to camp in the saloon every night. Soon
typhoid raged and twenty-five people died. What food there was, was
doled out in starvation rations. Twenty eight passengers attempted to
dine off the head of one sheep. Often the men, seeing how little there
was at meals for women and children, would walk away without eating
anything.

Four months after leaving England, New Zealand was sighted. To
everyone's horror the drunken skipper, Captain Dunn, made straight for
the coastal rocks. The passengers rebelled and voted to put him in leg
irons before shooting him. But a compromise was made. They drugged
him. As the first mate was drunk too, the second mate took charge.
Because of the typhoid, the ship was quarantined for three weeks and
so terrible was the filth on board that when the Health Officer, Dr.
Donald, boarded her at Lyttelton the port of Christchurch, he had to
turn up his trouser cuffs.

While at Lyttelton, Captain Dunn fell off the pier drunk and drowned
himself.

Thomas: (Repeatedly) Another girl.
My wife, Abigail 1, has never learned to stand on her head
immediately at the conclusion of conjunctio. Or is it that she
should jump up and down? I might by now have had a team of
labourers flexing toward puberty. Rebecca Abigail Martha Mary
Emily Eliza Jane Margaret Susan. Am I breeding tour guides?
This swamp I cannot drain alone. The Boyne leaks through all
the land, the land I was blessed to be born on and which now I
cannot sell. Soon it'll be helicopters patrolling the border and
bombs and shootings and bodies dragging up our front path to
use the phone and what if they were Catholic?
Christchurch. Church of Christ. And it's Protestant. That might
be just our cup of tea. I'm getting down on my knees to pray.
Christchurch though, they say it's a swamp. But at least it's a
swamp that's drained. We won't have to do it ourselves girls.

I'm taking nosodes to root out my ancestral leftovers. Syphilis,
plagues, typhoid, whatever my lineage, at 6PM peak time each day I

suck on my treatment. Sliced from the diseased tissue of a dead
body, a little goes a long way. This isn't my great grandmother I'm
chewing on. It could be anybody. This prescription isn't an order to
take one before meals and another before bed time. From 6pm I
have six hours to buffer myself against zombie invasion. Or the
zombie that might, by bed time, emanate from my own body and
loiter beside my bed with an instinct only for re-entry. My body; if it
is living or just resting, I'm not sure any more.

   Whenever I'd left the house I'd meet someone I'd never before
met who felt I was in urgent need of a psychic reading; in a pub, or
bending over a freezer in the supermarket. I collated the data. I'm
the sleeping beauty, they said, asleep for a hundred years inside my
castle. A forest of thorns having grown outside, my only hope was that
a prince would one day pass and feel nosy enough to commit himself
to days and nights of slashing away without blunting his sword.

   That's the Disney version. In the Grimms version, her mother-in-law
comes to live with them and she's a cannibal. Blocking out this
possible fate after the romance, I obsessed instead in my
matrilinear inheritance. I'm coming out as the end product of my
foremothers.

   I'm feeling what it means to be a foremother. While Herakles
chopped at the heads of the Hydra, up to his thighs in her swamp,
the she-crab pierced his ankle and would not let go. That kind of
mother. Force and will and eyeballs where a brain might otherwise
have been. I'm not a princess or a crab. I'm a Hydra, because a
Hydra has more eyes to rotate than a crab.

Christchurch. My street had been the reddest light street in the red
light district. The cottages are being demolished for a tour coach
park. Coach park first, then a high rise Holiday Inn.This will cut out
my view to the cemetery, segregated in death, Catholic from
Protestant. Too close to the river, the foundations of the cottages are
sagging into the swamp anyway. My view is straight across to the
cemetery over a field of concrete. (Only sensible.) The concrete and
the coaches will only sag in the end, so when they build their Holiday
Inn, that should sag too. Like the pock-holed cemetery, the holes are
the same size as bodies but without any bodies in them.

   At the end of the street, the Star and Garter, the knees-up before
staggering out to the river to drown, alternatively, to stagger out
along the red light street. Most nights a face is plastered on one of
my windows or a knock on my door for directions or now that your
door's open, is this the right place?

   I've taken to staying at home. The Hydra has anchored her curtains
at the lower corners so she doesn't scream when, behind their hot
breath the faces blur on her windows.

   Before the bridges, even no bridge to the cemetery, all the pubs
along the river had a morgue room to lay out the bodies of their

drowned clientele. I've got a spare room now and I might have to use it.

They weren't only knocking on the door, they were entering and pillaging. That's why I don't go out to work. I listen and my eyes rotate and I watch.

The soil on all sides of my cottage is choked with twitch. A root system that strangles everything, even itself. It likes a good swamp. It buttresses the swamp and that's why my cottage survives. The leaves of the twitch crack when it is under feet. I've trained myself to hear when the twitch cracks and where, and that's the route of the prowler.

I believed that Antonio, who was named after a saint, was doing me a favour. He'd ploughed up the twitch with a rotary hoe. An expert leaned over the gate to give her opinion.

She said, "If you're trying to breed twitch, that's a successful technique. That's division. It should be called multiplication. Chop off one inch of the root and you'll get a plant twenty feet across."

"She's so pretentious," said Antonio, "She has to overcompensate because she's dyslexic. And she's a Protestant."

She was right though.

He said I was pretentious because I want to do poncy things with my brains. I'm not a Protestant or a Catholic. Antonio hung a spotlight from the back porch and hoed and forked and raked until one in the morning. To me, that was pretentious. Finally he had to stop. Catholic or Protestant, he had to eat.

"Are you having a satisfying relationship with your vegetables?" I said.

"Yes."

I knew about relationships with plants. I'd had one. It was visual lust. Explosive. I planted in curves and I planted so the shapes and curves of the foliage would set each other off.

Antonio was silent for a week. He sulked until at the end of the week, while I was indoors doing something pretentious with my brains, he was digging out my plants and replanting them in rows. His pretensions were saintly. To save me the trouble later on. If he respected me, it was just enough to trust that later I'd recognise the error of my ways.

One night I had a vision. After something like sex, I saw lettuces that grew like cubes so they wouldn't waste space when they were packed in a box.

I come from a family of straight cement paths, dense lines of carrots cabbage beans onions potatoes lettuce tomatoes corn peas hens. I was trained to save paper bags and fold each segment of toilet paper twice. The nosodes didn't have to remind me. I bonded with ease to Antonio and he couldn't stop reminding me.

When he introduced me to his grandmother, the Irish, not the Italian one, she couldn't remember which one he was. She tested his response to the list of names she remembered. Her legs were bandaged from chopping down trees. You can't plant a straight line when there's one of those huge provocative rooted things right where it shouldn't be. He'd learned all he knew about waste not want not from his grandmother. Antonio's tomatoes were wasted. Flagrantly pulled out one night and squandered.

"Along the top of a high fence you have to cement broken bottles onto it, then you roll out the barbed wire. One metre from the fence you dig a trench and distribute more bottles along its length. Along the outer edge of the trench you roll out more barbed wire. Then you set up one spotlight at each corner of the fence. I'm taking my sleeping bag and I'm going to sleep out there every night."

I wanted to encourage him. He was speaking to me.

He didn't even say "the bastards" he just got on with the job.

He took two thousand cuttings from poplar trees and planted them one foot apart inside the boundary fence.

"Poplar trees grow three feet in one year," he said.

This was the passive aggressive plan.

Now they've grown up.

The neighbours don't like me. It's my foliage. Like I'm shaking out my dandruff over the boundary fence. All day, all I hear is sweep, sweep (tut) sweep, sweep, sweep, sweep (tut).

She watches from her window. Whenever a leaf drops she, Iris, runs out with her broom.

She shouts to her husband. "For Christ Sake! If you'd help me, I might be able to keep up."

But Dougie's a meditator. Or a scarecrow. He stands all day in the middle of their flawless lawn.

I'm sitting on the sofa where the wall used to be. I'm waiting for the kettle.

"Would you like a cup of tea?" With earsplitting calls like this, we don't need colourful plumage.

Antonio can call or I can call through a door and two walls. If it's me, I can call from the kitchen through nine thousand rows of corn onions beans tomatoes courgettes as well as the door and two walls.

Then Antonio will call back, "In a minute."

The air is still and cool. I'm reading a page turner. For goals and rewards I make cups of tea. Since the inside walls were demolished, I can hold on just that bit longer. But I don't want to be responsible for the ruin or loss of any more electric appliances. Especially the kettle. Antonio's mother gave the kettle to us to share and we do.

Antonio is shut in the bedroom where his rakes and hoes and hoes are staying. He practices with them but the sound is like the mutter of the triple footed snout drum his sister was trying to help him with.

"Do you want a cup of tea?"

"In a minute."

Communication like this serves to bind a couple together for a lifetime —*David Attenborough*.

I'm in the book, I'm suspense retentive, but I must leave the sofa. The kitchen is a belly of fog, the windows steamed in. The kettle has boiled to a fizz and I'll have to start again.

I think it's called pink champagne. It's pinky ginger. It's moving closer to the window. It's on a branch. It must be a cat. It's not Marmalade so it must be Sandy. He's named after George next door's Uncle Sandy. They met Uncle Sandy on their trip to Ireland.

Sandy shouldn't be outside at night in the cold. He's had an operation and his bottom's been shaven. I was shocked. His bottom was quite flat. I thought cats would at least have buttocks to prance up on their stilettos and drape their ostrich feathers over your face with. But like Uncle Sandy, Sandy's known for his common sense. For him, exoticism goes only as far as a taste for tropical fruit. He's not the sort of chap who'd even need to be reminded on a cold night to pull his singlet down over his kidneys.

He's pushing himself flat against the window. It's like a seizure. Through a window in daylight I saw a cat once having a seizure. I wipe at the steam. Pinky ginger. It's hairy and fleshy with large lewd yellow teeth and a tongue and it's steaming up the window where I've wiped and it's a face and I'm screaming and my scream isn't ending. I'm screaming from my lowest sphincter. Opera singers practise this way but I'm screaming out the roots from my scalp. I'm not practising and the full vertical surge of my intestines stretches thirty feet.

When I'm all cleared out, my brains slot back into place and I can run. I'm running because the face is running. I run for the door and out to the gate and into the street. The pinky ginger hair and flesh slides away over the dark field of concrete between the tour coaches and the river.

Antonio has torn himself away from his practice.

"Do you want a cup of tea?" I'm asking him without screaming.

"Yes."

"Did you hear me?"

"Yes. I want a cup of tea."

"Did you not hear me scream?"

"Yes. It was extremely loud and you screamed for a very long time so I just thought, oh she's just electrocuting herself again. You made me lose count. I was counting my seeds. I was nearly up to 42,500. Now I'll have to start again."

There isn't much hope of being electrocuted by anything other than during tea making. All the other appliances have been burgled or peed on by Sandy's foster brother Tinky. He lines up with the burglars. If he gets in first, he aims a precise line into the the toaster the heater both the speakers and into each button in a row along stop play record pause eject.

Before his next silence, Antonio had said, "The burglars, they know you're pretentious. They don't steal anything from me." But that was before the tomato catastrophe. The smell and the shape of those plants. One mustn't let one's imagination run away.

"You need a man." That's what the experts say to me now. As though I hadn't been doing my job more than adequately well as a Hydra. And my scream. I could put that on my CV.

What do I need in a man? I need a scarecrow. A man like Dougie. Two of them. Two Dougies for outside. One for the back and one for the front. Antonio wasn't scary enough for outside.

When his seed count reached a million I knew he had a long term plan. I could never again think of asking him if he might be so kind as to choose between me and a row of, for example, courgettes.

He'd said,"Don't throw away those tea bags, put them out in the sun to dry and then we can re-use them." All those yoghurt pots I'd eaten my way through since we'd met. "Don't throw those away, I can use those to start my seeds off in."

When I'd eaten my way through three million pots of yoghurt and he'd planted all the seeds, his expansion plan was ready.

I'm taking nosodes to root out my ancestral leftovers. If this was Ireland, every field would be a black and rotting stench. Over every field violent thunder storms, lightning and torrential rain flooded. Over these rotting fields an extraordinarily dense fog descended; cold and damp and without any wind. It was there the mother of my mother's mother was conceived.

It. I am it, a knotted turgid build-up. At the same moment, it's a seed at the magic moment of germination. At the same moment it's a foetus. I'm watching a film of it. From the top of the frame an amniotic sac comes down long and narrow and cut off by the frame. The furniture is elastic and translucent. Hammocks and slings. In Africa and South America and Asia babies are tied directly to their mother's bodies all day to simulate the womb furniture. Western babies have voted top marks to straight copies of these. They just can't be improved on.

I do have other furnishings. Around the walls I have waterbeds and sofas and cushions. They might even be edible. In the middle of the floor, in the middle of my soft furnishings, a mysterious kind of plughole is becoming apparent. There's something down there.

I'm beginning to worry this might be a stopover lounge or a curtained off cabin on a first class flight to—but I don't know if I'm meant to land. There are no cabin crew and no other passengers I can ask.

I don't have any headphones but I have a wonderful, neverending, intravenous food supply.

I have no worries whatsoever about where my next meal is coming from.

Trying to get back to this or trying to get forward to it. This isn't remembering because I tried all my life to remember. Everyone else seems to know about this too. The trying to remember.

Something about this reminded me. Absolutely and molecularly communicating with the earth, outside in a park I have a pee in the dark while under the moon that same night, I have a respectful relationship with a magnolia tree. No-one will ever tell me this is pretentious. Later, I'd like to be planted under a magnolia tree.

It, the germinating seed was planted in the dark and having germinated as a foetus, I sprout a pair of cotyledons beyond the top of the frame. At the same time I'm sprouting roots that are nervously spreading until they get a grip.

ROOTING

I cohabit this language with the English

It feels like sandpaper around my organs.
It's unwordable, that strong sensation of
mother-tongue deficiency :
The recurring dreams of cakes, tarts, turn-overs
delegated to represent home
whip up a delirious tremens of hunger
at any, unexpected hour.
On rainy nights when I feel safer
because it's less likely we'd be broken into,
I sleep with strange words and phrases like :
reticent, mellifluous and clip-joint
(what on earth do they clip there?)
They lodge themselves into my ribcage and
smother my accent into an amorphous hot lump.
Once I open my mouth everybody knows
I am an alien,
even Jane who mixes up
emaciated with emancipated.
I have miscarried my mother-tongue in the car park
behind Tesco.

Fluency   Eva Forrai

tHe aniMateD

Adam.j.Maynard.

Shelly was trying to get her fingernail

under the ringpull of a can of Coors

Extra Gold. She was muttering under

her breath as the ringpull continued

to make a dull clicking noise.

Shell had applied a brand new layer of polish to

her nails earlier that day, pillarbox red, and was reluctant to

exert real effort for fear of either chipping the polish or, the

worst case scenario, breaking one of her slender nails.

"Tits," she screamed, as her nail broke and the lager

flowed over the top of the can. Now her nail was

fucked and she had wasted half of her beer.

Sonic Youth's new record was blasting from the

stereo. "Turn that shit off now!" she yelled. Her friend

Pea, who had been screening a Super 8 film

against the living room wall, turned around slowly,

and crossed her legs. "What's with you today? You're

a real live wire lately."

Shell said sorry, it wasn't Pea's fault. Things had been getting to her lately, it was hard to envisage any kind of progress in her life at this time. Her nail breaking at that moment seemed to be the final straw. Maybe the nail breaking was a sign, maybe her perfect nails were a way to protect her identity. As long as her nails were perfect everything else was good too. When the nail broke, however, she felt she would have to take stock of what was going on in her life. In some ways it was a relief that this defence was no longer up.

Shelly hadn't been out all day. In fact she hadn't been out for the last 2 days. She found being outside fairly similar to being inside. Sitting on the couch all day had become a way of life. In her tv world, Deputy Dawg was moving and tragic. His attempts at being a good sheriff were always foiled. The raccoon always seemed to get a laugh out of him somewhere along the line. Why do people eat baked beans when they know exactly what they are going to taste like every time?

4 GOBLIN HAMBURGERS IN gravy

Duncan McLean

(The living room of a flat in Leith. Back of eleven on a Sunday morning. There's been a big party the night before: empty bottles and cans lie everywhere, and full ashtrays. Also lying on the floor, in front of the settee, is Spacko. He's asleep. Slumped along the settee, also asleep, is Rab. They're both fully dressed, looking wrecked. It gets lighter.)

Rab   Oooooohhhhhh.
Spacko   Aaaaaahhhhhh.
Rab   Ooohhh god.
Spacko   Jesus my head.
          (Pause.)
Rab   (Shading his eyes.) What's that over there, that...light?

Spacko   I'll have a deek. (He crawls over, opens a curtain: sun BURSTS in. He shuts the curtain immediately.) I think it's the sun.
Rab   Tell it to piss off, will you.
Spacko   I can't speak, my mouth's too dry. Which is amazing considering the amount of liquid I swallowed last night.
Rab   Aye, it was a good party right enough, I ken. And I'll tell you how I ken.
Spacko   How?
Rab   Cause I can't remember a fucking thing about it! (They laugh.) It must've been good.
Spacko   It was good.
Rab   It must've been.
Spacko   It was. Do you not even mind what you did with that bottle of bleach?
Rab   (Groping his scalp.) I didn't dye my hair, did I?
Spacko   Nah. You poured it into the punch.
Rab   Did I?
Spacko   Aye. Two bottles of white wine, a half of Malibu,

a carton of pineapple juice...and a litre of Domestos.

Rab Did anybody drink it?

Spacko Nah. Janice spotted you doing it and slung it down the sink. Just as well: it would've killed the buggers.

Rab It would've brought their teeth up a lovely white though.

(They laugh. Spacko is back sitting on the floor again. Out of nowhere there is a groan from behind the settee. This turns out to be Mud.)

Mud Oooooohhhhhh fuck.

Spacko Was that you Rab?

Rab No. I thought it was you.

Spacko No.

Rab It must've been the settee.

Spacko **Hold on, it's coming back to me now.**

Rab That's what you get for eating all those pakoras.

Spacko Listen: on my way back from the window thenow, I mind...I saw a body lying there.

Rab Behind here?

Spacko Aye, on the floor.

Rab A dead body?

Spacko Dead? How can you tell?

Rab Hold on. (He levers himself up, looks over the back of the settee, then lies back down again.) No, he can't be dead: he's just boked up on the carpet.

Spacko That's a relief. (Pause.) Here, I hope he's not going to choke on his own vomit.

Rab What?

Spacko **Ken, like Hendrix, man:** diced carrot down the gullet, choke choke, snuffs it.

Rab (Shouts.) Hey pal, are you okay, or are you drowning in your own puke?

Mud Fffuuuuccckkk ooofff.

Rab *Did you hear that?*

Spacko Ungrateful bastard!

Rab Here's me trying to be friendly and I get tellt where to go!

Spacko I reckon we should wait till he comes out of his coma... then kick his fucking head in.

Rab	What a way to go though, eh? (Shakes his head.) There's only one worse way to die than choking on your own vomit.
Spacko	Worse? What could be worse than choking on your own vomit?
Rab	Choking on somebody else's vomit. (They laugh.)
Spacko	Here, I'll tell you something though. I wouldn't mind choking on Kelly Cant's bodily fluids.
Rab	There's a good reason for that though.
Spacko	Aye, she's a fucking ride.
Rab	No. You're a fucking perv.
Spacko	But did you see her last night? That dress! Big tits hanging out like...
Rab	...like a pair of big tits. That's nothing new as far as Kelly Cant's concerned. Now if they'd been sticking out like...the fucking Scott monument, two fucking Scott monuments, that would've been... Not on show at all, that would've been news.
Spacko	I worry about you sometimes, man. You never even tried to get a bag off the whole night.
Rab	Here, just cause I've got some self respect!
Spacko	Just cause you've got a microscopic dick, more like.
Rab	I ken you, you radge. You're the type that's always shagging some bird on the bathroom floor at parties, while there's a queue halfway down the hallway bursting for a pish.
Spacko	Who tellt you about that?
Rab	Folk're banging on the door, "Come on, let us in," and you're banging your head on the lavvy pan, too pished to even get it up proper! If you think that's smart, Spacko, you're even fucking thicker than I thought.
Gary	(Appearing in the doorway. It's his flat, so he's been sleeping in bed, just got up.) The boy's thicker than three pints of condensed shit.
Spacko	Morning Gary.
Gary	See what I mean? It's quarter past twelve and he's still calling it morning.
Spacko	Just being civil, you cunt!
Gary	*Fuck off.*
Spacko	Keep your bastard moods to yourself.
Rab	Are you in a bastard mood, boss?
Gary	Get your feet off my furniture or I'll stab you.

Rab (Moving his feet off the settee.) Sweetness and light.

Gary (Sitting on the settee.) Well look at the mess of the flat! Christ, I'm kind enough to invite the lot of yous round for a bit of a ceilidh, and what happens? You **trash** the bloody place!

Spacko Well at least you ken it was a good party.

Rab It was good. It must've been...

Spacko ...he can't remember a fucking thing about it! Come on, let's give Gary a hand to clean the place up a bit. (He starts picking up cans, shaking them, drinking the dregs.)

Rab See that? The bugger's pinching my punchlines now.

Gary Talking of pinching, did you ken I caught some bastard walking out the door with my video last night?

Rab What, had you not paid the rent on it, like?

Gary No, he was just fucking choring it—right in the middle of the party!

Rab So what did you do to him?

Gary I took the fucker out onto the balcony...and I tipped him over.

Rab What! Two floors up?

Gary Well, I made sure there was grass below first.

Spacko (Who's just drained a can.) Fuck! I think I've just drunk the ashtray!
(Rab and Gary laugh, then there is another groan from behind the settee.)

Mud Shut the racket, you cunts.

Gary What was that?

Rab I've been meaning to tell you Gary: there's a body on the floor behind the settee.

Gary That would explain it. (Pause.) Who is it?

Rab No idea.

Spacko Tell you one thing about him though.

Gary What?

Spacko He's just newly spewed his ring on the carpet.

Gary Oh no... (Goes to look, but stops.) I can't look.

Rab No need to: you can smell it from here.

Gary This is what happens. You move into a new flat, have a house-warming, and the joint gets fucking wrecked! Curtains pulled off the walls, lavvy blocked and the bog half-flooded, fags left burning the paintwork on the windowsills...and now some bastard puking up on the carpet that's not even paid for yet. Jesus fucking grat. At least when you puked, Rab, you had the sense to get most of it into the kitchen sink and not on the floor.

Rab   (Surprised.) Me? I didn't puke, did I?

Spacko   What's that down the front of your shirt then?

Rab   Aw shite!

Gary   (Jumping up.) Shite's the word, Rab, and we're in it if we don't sort this mess afore Janice gets up.

Spacko   She wasn't very keen on the party from the start, eh no?

Gary   She thought it'd turn out rowdy and the place would get trashed just after she'd finished doing it up.

Spacko   What a thing to think.

Gary   I tellt her: it'll only be a few mates, a couple dozen folk like. A few cans, a pot of curry on the go in case the *munchies* strike later on...

Rab   Here, I remember that curry. Most of it went over the kitchen wall.

Gary   Aye, and down the back of the cooker. It'll be lurking there now, waiting for Janice to go through in her baffies. Then it'll leap out and clart her ankles and she'll go completely mental. At me!

Rab   (Spotting Spacko trying to sneak out.) Here, where are you creeping off to?

Spacko   For a pish. And I expect the place spotless afore I get back. (He leaves.)

Gary   I mean, as if it was my fault it got a bittie out of hand.

Rab   No, it wasn't you doing the fucking can-can on the kitchen table or anything, was it?

Gary   Fair enough, I was in pretty high spirits.

Rab   The spirits were in you, more like. What was that you were on? Bells and Lambrusco slammers?

Gary   Don't start: I saw you getting wired into a **pint of Buckfast and Bacardi** at one point.

Rab   Here, I've just remembered: it was you that was chucking the curry all over the shop in the first place!

Gary   Eh... (Thinks.) Might've been.
        (As he says this, Mud starts to get up from behind the settee. He's wearing glasses and a leather jacket.)

Rab   Were you not in some kind of pagger?

Gary	Ah, hold on...aye. (Mud is standing behind them, rubbing his face, stretching.) I mind now: there was some guy'd tried to get off with Janice or something. Aye, that was it. He'd tried to pull her into the lobby cupboard with him.
Rab	Was that some speccy cunt? (Mud takes his specs off.)
Gary	Aye, don't ken who he came with like—no friend of mine. Anyhow, Janice tells him to fuck off, but he's still pestering her, and here's me walking by. So I tellt him to fuck off— and he tries to start a discussion about it! Arguing with me whether he can shag my wife or not! So I just chucked him out the door.
	(Mud looks—holding his specs up for a second—for the door, then starts to crawl towards it.)
Rab	Or tried to.
Gary	Aye, and while I was trying we ended up in the kitchen, and then the curry ended up on the fucking lino!
Rab	What a bastard, eh.
Gary	Totally out of order. I'll tell you, I'm going to stitch that prick if he shows his face again. Glasses, aye, and...did he not have a leather jacket on?
	(Mud takes off his leather jacket, rolls it up, hides it.)
Mud	No, he wasn't wearing a leather jacket.
Rab	Jesus Christ.
Gary	The dead have arisen.
Rab	How are you feeling now pal?
Mud	Ach, A1, A1. Fact I reckon I'll just, eh, shoot the crow.
Gary	Do you ken this radge in the glasses and jacket then?
	(Mud is edging towards the door, but Gary gets up and stops him.)
Mud	No no, not at all, I just saw him at the party, ken. Barrie party by the way, magic. Anyway, I'll be off...
Gary	Do I ken you?
Mud	Not exactly, eh...Gary, is it no? Friend of a friend more like. Kelly Cant, ken, I came with her.
Gary	I bet you did.
Rab	Here, better not let Janice hearing you calling this man a friend of Kelly's: too risky!
Gary	Did you see if she went off with anybody in the end?
Rab	If?
Gary	Well, who?
Mud	Me? Naw. I never saw nothing. I was blind drunk, ha ha!

Rab	You need glasses pal.
Mud	What? Glasses? Never. I don't ken what you're talking about.
Gary	Settle, settle, he was only joking. Jesus, listen: what we all need is a good strong...
Rab	**...belt of whisky!**
Gary	Well if you can find any, Rab, you're welcome to it, cause I tell you, I'm never drinking again.
Mud	Neither am I, never. Well, not till thenight, anyroad.
Gary	No, what I was going to say was coffee, I'll make some coffee, wake us all up a bit.
Rab	Tell you what man, I'll get it, I'll get the coffee. You and, eh, Smiler here, you get started on the clearing up.
Mud	He gets the good job, eh!
Rab	Well it's like this, to be honest: I'd find it hard to sort out the junk around here from the good stuff. For a start I'd chuck out most of Gary's CDs. UB40? Straight in the fucking binbag! (He leaves.)
Gary	What a chancer, eh? Right, no time to waste... (Jumps to his feet, looking around.) Let's get started.
Mud	I was thinking I might just be going actually.
Gary	**Like hell you will.** Clearing up is the price you pay for gatecrashing my party and then dossing down in my living room—without even asking me!
Mud	I would've asked you if I'd kent I was going to sleep here, but I just kind of fell into a coma all of a sudden, I didn't have time to get a hold of you.
Gary	Here, get a hold of this. (Gives him a sup from the dregs in a bottle of voddy, then shouts:) Hurry up with the coffee, Rab, we're parched in here. (Suddenly realising:) Oh fuck, I hope I haven't woken Janice.
Mud	**Wife got a bit of a temper, has she?**
Gary	I won't have a word said against her, the ill-natured bitch.
Mud	She seemed fine enough to me last night.
Gary	(Staring at him.) What do you mean by that?
Mud	Eh...nothing.
Gary	You ken, your face is starting to look a bit familiar to me.
Spacko	(Entering.) **Fuck me, who's this?**
Gary	I was just about to ask, Spacko.

Mud	Eh, I'm the body from behind the settee, actually.
Spacko	I guessed that much pal, but what's your name?
Mud	Call me Mud.
Spacko	Shite!
Gary	Eh?
Mud	Not, really. Well, not really really. My real name is Alexander, Sandy for short. So you see Sandy, eh...Earth, eh...Mud! My name is Mud.
Rab	(Entering quickly.) Here, lads: bad news.
Spacko	What?
Gary	Where's the coffee?
Rab	That's the bad news: no hot water, so no coffee.
Gary	No hot water?
Spacko	Heat some up in the kettle you daft cunt.
Rab	The kettle's fucked.
Gary	No.
Rab	I was away to plug it in, when I saw this brown gunge clogging up the socket. Then I realised, it's the same brown gunge that's all over the cooker and the kitchen wall: that fucking curry's got everywhere, man.
Mud	Could you not have used a knife or something, poked the curry out of the socket?
Rab	Now that's a bright idea. (Acts ELECTROCUTION.)
Spacko	Come on lads, I'm starving. How am I supposed to get working on this mess on an empty stomach?
Gary	What this? Keen to do some clearing up all of a sudden after skiving off for half an hour?
Spacko	What? Against the law to have a good long pish now, is it?
Rab	Good long wank, more like.
Spacko	Fuck off. I just had a pish, quick rinse of the face, tried to mind what's on Scotsport this afternoon.
Rab	Hazel Irvine's on Scotsport, you bastard: you were having a wank.
Gary	I hope you cleaned the sink after you finished, man. Janice hates a dirty sink.
Spacko	Here, Gary, can your cock 'touch' your 'arse?
Gary	Heh, no bother.
Spacko	Well away and fuck yourself.
Rab	Ah-ha!

Spacko	Better still, away and make us some **bacon and eggs**, you bastard. A few slices of toast each, beans, maybe...
Gary	And how am I going to do that with the kitchen electrics fucked?
Spacko	Okay then, cornflakes and fucking milk, bread and bloody jam—just hurry up afore I drop with hunger, right?
Gary	Your wish is my command, oh great Master...bator. (Leaves.)
Mud	I won't bother with breakfast actually folks, don't have the stomach for it, so eh...

(Mud's about to say goodbye, when Gary runs back in, angry.)

Gary	Okay Rab, very funny, let's end the joke now.
Rab	**Eh?**
Gary	I thought you were taking a long time making the coffee if the kettle wasn't working. Now where is it?
Rab	The kettle? On the unit.
Gary	No, not the fucking kettle. The food! Where's all the food gone?
Rab	What are you talking about?
Gary	I'm talking about some bastard's taken all the food out of the cupboard, and the fridge as well—**fucking walked off with all my grub!**
Spacko	Rabbo wouldn't do that, Gary.
Gary	You, you radge! I'm going to check the bog. (Gary rushes out. The others look at each other, shrug. Gary reappears.)
Gary	Aw fuck. (CLUTCHING HIS HEAD.) And Janice just went out yesterday and bought in about twenty quids worth. Pies, cheese, tins of tuna...
Mud	Nothing to do with me, mate.
Gary	I ken, I ken, you've been here the whole time, you're definitely not the guilty party.
Rab	That'll be it man: the party. Folk get hammered, get hungry. There's always some gutsy bugger starts raiding the kitchen cupboards.
Spacko	Probably the curry would've done them...
Rab	...if it hadn't been for that speccy cunt starting trouble and spilling it.
Mud	Listen lads, I'm away...
Spacko	Aye Mud, you go and check, see if Gary's maybe missed

something at the back of the cupboard.

Mud (Reluctantly.) Aye, okay. (He leaves.)

Gary To take the whole lot! A whole week's food! Janice'll kill me...and then we'll starve to death. Sometimes life is just...

Rab # Shite.

Gary ...just...

Spacko ## Shite.

Gary ...not worth the hassle.

Mud (Running back in, grinning.) Lads, lads, we're saved, they haven't taken everything!

Rab Thank Christ.

Mud They left something.

Spacko *What is it?*

Mud # A   T I N .

Spacko Open it quick, I'm wasting away here.

Gary **A   t i n   o f   w h a t ?**

Mud 4 Goblin Hamburgers In Gravy! (Everybody cheers.) Can I have complete silence, please, while I perform the traditional Opening Of The Tin Ceremony.

(Mud kneels down in front of the settee, takes out a can-opener, and slowly, slowly, opens the tin. They all look into it for a second, sniffing, grinning. Then Mud takes four forks out of his pocket, and gives them out, a burger speared on the end of each one. They raise the burgers in a kind of toast to each other, then eat them, savouring every mouthful.)

Spacko These are fucking magic by the way.

Rab (Nodding at Mud.) Aye, compliments to the chef.

Mud Who cares about the fucked cooker? These are better cold.

GARY # Aaaaaahhhhh. Life is good.

(They finish eating, lay their forks down, and lean back on the settee and the floor. They're well fed and satisfied. The lights go down.)

EL FNA

JOE AMBROSE

I'd love to say I love you but the
CIA are listening. I'm on a card phone
and the hustlers are all around me trying to
sell me extra time on their cards. They don't do a bad deal. I
don't know how they turn a profit. You use their card and give
them cash for the time you've used. I don't believe one can
buy time. You're in your room back in the West in the big city.
I'm on the side of the Post Office in Marrakesh, on the side of
the righteous. I miss you but I'm taking my life into my own
hands. The hustlers are not so tough. They're just poor boys
entitled to rob the rich.

I have two bootleg cassettes back in my hotel. One by
Gregory Isaacs, another by Peter Tosh. In the 70s when I first
listened to the reggae music it moved my soul. All the music
in Marrakesh is bootleg. Lowgrade cassettes with color
photocopy covers. Most of the tapes are Rai, the Algerian
disco music that sounds fruity and cheesy. As a boy I wanted
to be Johnny Too Bad. As a man I became him.

So I say goodbye to you on the phone. Just at the moment
of farewelling, I miss you the most. I'm like a monk who has
taken vows, but as you might imagine they're spiritual not
physical vows. The desert here is arid and orange.   When I
drive through it I feel erotic. I feel at home here and that is

I move faster.

"Do you not remember me my friend?"

Up ahead I see the Militaire approach. My hustler has disappeared.

**

Paul Bowles has a short story about a man walking through Place Djemma El Fna. The man, Ben Tajaj, paused, looked to the ground, and spotted a sealed envelope bearing his name and address. He picked up the envelope, went to a cafe on the border of the Place, and opened it. The note inside read: "The sky trembles and the earth is afraid, and the two eyes are not brothers."

We booked into the CTM Hotel. Three of us. Me the oldest. The youngest a kid from England called Cousin. "We" is me and Traven. We've worked together for seven years.

Place Djemma El Fna means "The Place of The Mosque for The End of The World." They used to behead people in the centre of the square. Later they would hang the heads of victims on spikes around the square's perimeters. These days El Fna is full of hustlers and whores and drug people. Radi the pseudo-Gnoua who is really a dope dealer. He has all these photographs of fat American girls he obviously fucked one holiday long ago. He must have looked good one time but now he looks rattled and scared. Sometimes I think he has AIDS but I find him pretty useful. He gets things for me.

El Fna is vast, dusty, windy, bordered by the Medina, the mosques, the endless coffee shops and cafes. Snobby cafes where they'd never serve us when we were with the Gnoua. A clean respectable one, not unlike the Cafe De Paris in Tangier, allowed the Gnoua to join us. There was a deeply disreputable dive that never closed. Cafe Zagora. Home to whores and queers and junkies and thieves and sex kids. In this particular cafe Marrakesh became Sextown. I saw the infection everywhere. In the eyes of the beautiful children, in the dirty talk of the street women, in the garage of the CTM Hotel where a ten year old boy offered me a blow job for ten dirhams. "Ten dirhams," he said without confidence, indicating with his right hand and his mouth what was on offer.

I moved from cafe to cafe all day, always ending up in Cafe Zagora. The same old tramp always slept at the same table in the corner. He wore a ragged old brown djellaba which suggested, maybe, that he was at one time a musician. A djellaba is the traditional mode of dress in Morocco, the full-length garment with the peaked hood that often appears in tourist photos. It's a garment of great sophistication and beauty. For the tramp in Cafe Zagora his torn djellaba was the last relic of respectability.

The Plumber was the King of Zagora. He approached me the first night I went there. He told me that I had beautiful white skin, a kind lie, and that he was The Plumber of Marrakesh, famous for clearing out people's pipes. He was in his late thirties, full of human energy, and his sweaty demeanour suggested that he'd undertaken one plumbing job too many.

"I will clear out your pipes for you, my friend. Anytime. I know many times Mick Jagger, he have very big house near here," he said. Sightings of various Rolling Stones, living and dead, are common in Morocco, but The Plumber was useful at times. Like all lowlifes he has what they call in Morocco "Special Information".

The myriad daytime eating houses and neutral meeting places were the sites, overt and covert, of our assignations with the Gnoua, Sufi street kids in street gangs. The Gnoua organized our trips to the deserts. They acted as our hosts. The desert drugs, obscure, discreet and crazy, let me hear the music of the desert in my heart. In Marrakesh we were always at CTM, an old bus company hotel preserved from the epoch of Garbo and Clark Gable.

**

I woke each day to the sound of snake charmers playing badly on rhaitas. When I was ready to roll I'd stroll out onto the CTM balcony for coffee and orange juice. The balcony has the greatest view in the world, the Atlas snow-capped mountains looming triumphantly over the ancient city, a David Lean perspective come to life in the morning. I'd sit at a table looking out over El Fna, reading any old rubbish by way of a battered paperback.

The reason I went to Marrakesh was to look for paintings by the Canadian painter Brion Gysin. He lived in Morocco for thirty years, and his best works were delicate calligraphic studies of El Fna. Most of the sketches for those works were done on the balcony where I took my breakfast. I'd been told by a dodgy art dealer in London that there was an English guy living in Marrakesh who had about ten Gysins and who urgently needed money. He'd had a good life in Morocco, living cheaply and well. Now he'd been hit by the plague and the cash had run out. He wanted to return to England to die, said the art dealer.

By the time we reached Marrakesh he'd been dead for three weeks. His house had been stripped by his retainers, and our long work of reclaiming the Gysins had begun. We had other business on El Fna. Money was not the problem or the issue. We came to Marrakesh to be in the ancient city and to do stuff there.

Cousin's folks were rich English Catholics happy to indulge his foppish tastes and his lowlife aspirations. I think they gave him money to stay away. He looked like that kind of English boy. Blonde and tall and thin like a textbook example of the type. Cousin wanted to take a lot of drugs in Marrakesh. Opium, LSD, and Hashish. Drugs made him feel good. Traven wanted to collect on his DAT recorder the music of Gnoua. I was looking for art, other art, and anything that moved. We didn't have a whole lot in common other than our basic crookedness. They were my employees. The art world is a criminal world. I'd pay for a painting if I had to, but could never think of art as being one man's property. Property is theft, said one of the old-line Anarchists. There are many ways to acquire art in Morocco.

There's this painting of Gnoua that I'd really love to have. The title is Fete à Alger, and it features 19th Century Gnoua in Algeria. Playing in a pillared courtyard, similar to courtyards I've seen in Gnoua palaces in Marrakesh. The artist was Albert Girard. He specialized in black dancers and black musicians. What demon sent Albert looking for the dark heart of the Gnoua? And what did he fancy by way of diversion? And did he die out here on the fringe?

Marrakesh is an equivocal place but all the time that we were there the first people to greet us each morning, the last to see us before we went to bed at night, were the Gnoua. Each morning I'd wait for Hassan on the CTM balcony, the perfect place for reading, looking, waiting.

**

I look over the balcony and Hassan is standing there. He is holding his bike and waving to me, laughing. He speaks good French and Berber and Bambara (the language of the Gnoua), but poor English. I have perfect English and about 20 words of French.

"Where is your friend?" he shouts.

"He is in his bedroom sleeping," I shout back to him. "Why don't we meet up on the Place in an hour?"

"Is no problem," says Hassan as he prepares to leave.

My "friend" is Traven, who busies himself with Hassan and his musicians. Traven took a lot of acid and went to a lot of raves. He got into trance music. Then he got into the

spiritual trance music of Goa. And then he got to know the trance of Morocco.

Hassan moves away slowly. He looks back and waves to me. I wave back. My fellow hotel guests, mainly Europeans, look to me darkly as we share the balcony. Why am I shouting to the 16 year old black boy with the bike down below me on El Fna? Why is he shouting back to me?

Hassan is direct in his dealings and makes me behave the same way.

The day passes on El Fna. Coffee with Gnoua. Hustle with the hustlers. Radi wants to sell me a consignment of dope. He thinks I'm really a drug smuggler and he obviously has no sympathy for contemporary European art. Radi is a thief and, this being the case, knows how to find stolen stuff. He's priceless. So far he has reclaimed 2 Gysins. One reclamation turned nasty and, Radi said, there was some blood. I gave him an extra 500 dirhams.

In the morning I cross El Fna in Western gear. Levi shirt and combats and Ray Bans and Swatch. A Gnoua woman, her face covered with a black veil, whispers into my ear: "The Gnoua will never accept you because you refuse to wear the djellaba." In the late afternoon, after a shower, I hit the square anew. I bump into the Gnoua lady again. This time I wear an expensive djellaba made in the Rif mountains from raw wool. A notable item. She holds her black veil rather theatrically over her face: "The Gnoua will never accept you even though you disguise yourself in the djellaba." She is a beautiful woman and what she really wants to do is to sell me drugs or sex. She is the Berber Bitch of mythology. The Gnoua are the Whirling Dervishes of legend.

The day is confusing. I can't find Cousin. Traven tells me that he saw the boy at lunchtime.

"He said he had a suss on one of the paintings," says Traven, smoking a joint in his bedroom. He lies on his bed naked, only gradually covering his cock and balls with a paper thin sheet.

"Radi is going crazy bringing shit to me," I say to Traven. "All art known to man. He brought me a shitty print of The Boy In Blue last week. And some nice Moroccan stuff that was pretty cheap."

"He robs the stuff," says Traven, inhaling and gushing.

"Of course he fucking robs the stuff. He probably kills grannies to get it," I say, laughing. "There is a funny side to his desperation. He has this ancient t-shirt I'd really like to have which must come from Israel. As far as I can make out it supports some far-right Zionist gang. He must've gotten it from some Jewish bitch he was fucking. I've offered him ok money for it lots of times but he's kind of strange about it."

"He sure is kind of human," says Traven as he gets up from the bed and looks for his jeans, "and he gets through a heap of lowlifes every day."

"Yeah," I say. "I just wish Cousin would show up."

"Probably having the time of it with some sweet child," says Traven, who thinks optimistically about sex.

An hour later we go to eat in a European restaurant. Traven wants to go see the Gnoua in the square. He wants to tape them right away. They play the best in the dark. At night the atmosphere changes radically, and the forces of the diabolic are occasionally summoned up. We eat, pay our bill, and leave. I go back to the Hotel with Traven to pick up the DAT machine. We go to Cousin's room and knock on his door. No sound. No lights.

In the evening El Fna is fast. We go to the part of the square where Hassan works with his troupe. We sit in the dirt with the players, a gas-lit lamp illuminating our rebel stance. Hassan urgently instructs one of his friends to get us some mats and some tea. The food vendors light up their barbecues and the wind blows the smoke in our direction. The music gets crazy and I look up to see a star-filled sky. I look over at Hassan. He is a 16 year old boy with balls. He is surrounded by rumour, the curse of the enigmatic, and his face is full of anger and hurt when he sings.

**

We never saw Cousin again. We stayed at the CTM for three more weeks. Searching for him and searching for Gysins. We got two more paintings. Radi came up with one, and I discovered one myself. In the days after his disappearance Traven and me talked about Cousin all the time. We discussed his sexuality and we recalled minor adventures we'd had together; the train journey from Tangier to Marrakesh across the deserts, nights at Cafe Zagora, drugs he liked the most.

Three months before we'd picked him up in London. Traven met him in a club and got his number. A mutual friend introduced them. The next day Cousin rang and I told him I wanted a Third Man to accompany me and Traven to Morocco for sex and theft.

"What qualifications are necessary?" he said, adolescent and tough.

"A fuck-you attitude to Western Civilisation and an affection for its art," I said.

"Oh well," he laughed, "I'm afraid to say you've found your man."

The three of us met up at a cafe near the British Museum later the same day. He had long blonde hair, over six foot tall, milk-fed aristocratic product of English money. Cousin lived with his mother in Notting Hill, was haughty, rich, handsome. He proved a brave soldier during our travels. When he was missing for three days I went to talk with the Hotel manager. He had a large salubrious office right behind the CTM Reception. He had middle-aged in his blue blazer. His good job made him cautious about me and my gang.

"I think my English friend has returned to London," I said trying to sound pompous like a European. "He left some of my things in his room. If you give me the key to his room I'll get my stuff and fix up with you for whatever he owes you."

"Certainly, sir," said the manager. I'd been imperious and mentioned the possibility of money, a combination that makes Moroccans jump to attention.

Traven and me unlocked the door full of worry but, inside, everything was normal. Cousin just walked out that door, expecting to return later that same day. I filled his bag with his stuff, looked around. He'd been reading the English historian AJP Taylor, and keeping a diary. There was nothing for us to worry about in the diary, nothing that gave a clue as to why he'd disappeared. There were poems, extracts from books he'd been reading, things he'd heard on the radio. The last entry, a poem, contained the one morsel of intelligence that illumined his departure:

The heart will not agree.
10 dirhams to go with me.
At the side of the CTM Hotel
El Fna, Marrakesh,
Between Heaven and hell.

**

The Plumber told me what happened to the blonde English boy in the dark deserted alleyways of the Marrakesh Medina. It was the day before our departure when we spoke. He apologized for not having conveyed the information to me before this. He'd just spent two weeks locked up in the police jail which exists, an underground fortress, beneath the ground on Place Djemma El Fna. It was in the prison that he heard what became of Cousin. What he told me was the cause of our departure.

"I meet this bastard down below in the Police. He be bad bastard, and he be with your friend," said The Plumber. "Your friend meet him in Zagora, and be talking about these photographs you look for. The photographs of the dead English Zemmel. The bastard told your friend that he understood perfectly where these things go. He be Zemmel himself! He like very young boys. He say he get boys for the English Zemmel before he die. He know the boy who stole the paintings perfectly. Your friend he was very happy! So the next day he go to Banque Moroccaine de Afrique and he get a lot of money! Your friend have a very good credit card! I don't know the next thing that happened. Your friend going to meet the man with the photographs in the park of the Grand Mosque. When he get there he meet a lot of people. A lot of people there! They grab him, they kick him down, they know all the money, they take it off him. He was hit with the knife one time making a lot of blood everywhere! The bastard from the Police tell me all this stuff! He be there!"

"Did they kill him?" I asked.

"No. Some woman took him away to her place in the Medina. She be very good holy woman! He die later."

**

I ran into Hassan as I crossed El Fna looking for a taxi.

"You go now?" he said, looking worried as usual.

"Yes. My friend has died," I said. I looked him straight in the eye. He had this information already.

"Yes," he said. " Your friend must have had a very good idea for himself."

"He must have had." I smiled.

He walked me to a taxi. I put my bags in the boot, rummaged through one of them, found the Peter Tosh tape. I handed it to him. He looked at it quizzically. Hassan exists on El Fna.

Traven remained on El Fna for 24 hours. We met up back in London three weeks later.

**

I wish it was four weeks ago. I was on a card phone and my units were coming to an end. The hustlers were looking over my shoulder. They knew my time was up. They pushed their cards in front of my face. They told me that I could pay later when I was finished. But I'm a conservative guy. I believe in paying now not later. So I said goodbye to you and you said the same to me. I told you that I'd see you in a month and that was no lie.

PiNg poNg GaMe

Adam.j.Maynard.

Sand scrunched under people's feet, children were screaming and playing. There were beach balls, armbands, dinghys, lilos, and brightly coloured inflatable beach toys. Pea could hear the sea in the distance with its calming waves. Fun and relaxation were the order of the day, worries could take a back seat for a while.

Pea had just been for a refreshing dip and was now laid out on her beach towel, drying in the warm sunshine. After she had applied a little Soltan to her arms, neck and face, she put on her sunglasses and placed the lotion back in the hot sand. Something wasn't quite right though. The bottle didn't feel as though it was in the correct position. It felt awkward. She would have to move it. It bugged Pea that after all this time there were still hints that her disorder of years gone by was to a slight extent still with her.

As she looked up at the bright sky, she tried to think of why she felt compelled to move certain objects. Maybe it was a way of grounding herself. As she began to doze, Pea considered the notion that home exists in the head. If she could order the things around her, maybe she would be able to slow down the thoughts in her head.

Click/click, ping-pong, pong-ping, click/click, back and forth, back and forth, back and forth, back and forth.

A small wooden house had been built for her on the far side of their lawn. It was about five feet tall with windows and a proper roof made out of grey slate. She stood there in her green dress, staring directly at the camera across a garden strewn with golden leaves. The shutter opened and closed quickly, click/click, as she looked up to the kitchen window. Inside, her mother struggled with a can of tuna and muttered underneath her breath. Looking from the door of her 'little' house, Pea realised that she knew her property intimately. She had absorbed almost every detail of its sole room. She felt safe there, and found that she could immerse herself in her own private world.

In her real house she said goodnight to her favourite things as if they could hear. She spoke to her collection of plastic animals and people as if they were friends. Her particular favourite was a small, plastic, orange bear. His friendly gaze made him trustworthy, but just as likely she loved him because orange was her favourite colour.

Pea's bear sometimes spoke to her. He asked if she was happy, or what she had been up to that day. As time went by though, the bear became less real. It appeared to be losing its soul. The paint for its eyes, nose and mouth started to peel and chip away. Her heart felt empty, but the bear still meant something to her.

Clack/clack, ping-pang, pang-ping, clack/clack, back and forth, back and forth, back and forth, back and forth.

Pea slowly came around from her shallow sleep. She felt curiously detached, but was unsure what this feeling meant. Her new dreams were disturbing, but liberating at the same time. It was time to get her house in order, it had become untidy and confused, dishevelled and unkempt. It wasn't going to be easy...

Apples and angels. Bumble bees and bloody arms. Calcium and chocolate.Death and destruction. Eggplants and eucalyptus. Figs and fenugreek. Gall bladder and gin. Hunger and hitchcock. Idiots and iggy pop. Jasmine and jism. Killing and killjoys. Lunatics and languages. Manners and masturbation. Nightmares and nothingness. Orgasms and ornaments. Ping-pong and penises. Qualms and quakes. Red and rag. Salad and semen. Television and torment. Ugly and unusual. Vacant and vagabond. Witch and water. Xylophone and x-ray specs. Yelp and yahoo. Zebra and zero.

Pea knew the task ahead was mammoth, but at the same time she relished the thought of a calmer, less muddled mind.

HOMELAND

Mark Delaware

Questioner: Tell me about your obsession with the Heath at Hampstead.

Narrator: Oh come off it. We hardly know each other.

Questioner: OK. Is your childhood a good place to start? Or maybe you could tell me about coming out.

Narrator: Yes, I should start there. Indulge in a little self-reflection; most writers do.

Questioner: Well, describe the scene: read out what you've written.

Narrator: A sugary love poem sits in the drawer of a pine table in a suburban home somewhere in the early 80s. Beside the table, an adolescent sits reading about Aztec Camera in *Smash Hits* while jotting down phrases such as 'love means nothing' and 'my pain feels like a cloak of darkness'.

'What a poem,' the adolescent thought, 'and what a life.' This was the fifth poem he'd penned that week about the symbolism of dead trees; he was, after all, studying the Romantic Poets for A Level. And yet, he knew he could be more interesting.

Questioner: And could he?

Narrator: Oh yes. He'd probed into his personality for the first time while inserting a soap-lubed finger (a dextrous one at that, for he had passed Grade 6 Piano) into his anus during a racey bout of masturbation.

'I'm gay,' he gasped, in a high-pitched shrill like Jimmy Somerville. 'I must be a sensitive soul,' he added in a David Sylvian tone.

He positioned himself with his legs slung over his shoulders (like Marc Almond might do on a good night) so as to bring his penis nearer his mouth. He sucked at it like a child does when they cut their finger for the first time; nervously at first, but then more hungrily.

'I'm gay,' he thought, 'I must have interesting neuroses, effervescent wit and indecently good taste.' (He later discovered he was right on one count: he was neurotic.) He stood in front of the mirror and touched his milky arse with his spare hand. 'I'm gay,' he said again. 'I am destined to become a fashion designer or a careworker.'

'Or a cake bloody maker or a hairdresser,' added his Catholic mother helpfully as she came in to pick up his laundry.

Little globs of joy bubbled onto the purple carpet; they marked his flight from heterosexual captivity. Sprinkled on the shag pile, the sperm resembled fun snow at a suburban party. He stared at it proudly and felt re-born. He flicked a finger of spunk into his mouth and wondered: Did Genet beat off with his fingers jammed up there?

Questioner: Why are you trying to hide yourself behind humour?

Narrator: It's my tragi-comic psyche.

Questioner: Can't you just be truthful?

Narrator: I'd prefer truth.

Questioner: So can we move on to the Heath? What do you think about as you traipse around up there?

Narrator: Last time I went, I thought of a gay barbecue set amid the trees. Madonna and Kylie were there.

Questioner: Why did you invite them into your mind?

Narrator: Because I was scared.

Questioner: But what can they do for you?

Narrator: They make me, indeed they make many gay men happy.

Questioner: Would they go to the Heath?

Narrator: Of course. Since Madonna's career, like her waist, has sagged dramatically she has needed to address the pink pound more directly.

'Gays are the best fucks. I love to lick inside their tight, liver-like arseholes,' she wailed, laughing like a banshee.

On that occasion, Kylie was more philosophical: 'In a wardrobe of straight dresses your gay friend is that one little satin slip dress,' she giggled, rather annoyingly.

Questioner: Of the two, who do you prefer?

Narrator: Madonna.

Questioner: Did Madonna and Kylie slip from your mind when the action hotted up?

Narrator: Yeah. In my fantasy, they got pissed off with being stuck in my mind.

'It's getting too hot in here,' Madonna complained.

Cramped by the limitations of my

psyche, Ms Minogue relieved her boredom with an E while Madonna took a Latino boy behind a tree to finger-fuck him to orgasm. She returned from behind the tree and wiped her finger clean on a red picnic napkin.

Madonna didn't like Kylie being there. 'For fuck's sake, first I get stuck in some fuckwit's mind and then he puts me in a goddam Irvine Welsh fantasy with Kylie Minogue.'

Questioner: So what happened next?

Narrator: I put something naff and dancey on the tape machine of my mind. For 5 minutes, the Heath became a deconsecrated Church, my body a private chapel, my mind the altar on which Madonna could fuck Jesus.

Questioner: That is a little hysterical, isn't it? Does this mean you're in awe of Madonna?

Narrator: Absolutely. I even asked for her autograph at the barbecue. She signed the shit-smeared napkin for me.

Questioner: And did you speak to Kylie?

Narrator: No. By the time I got to her, she was hugging everybody in that way floored stars do.

La Ciccone detested Kylie.

'You know what gets me,' she thundered. 'The way women like you look at me. I mean, is it a fucking crime that I'm getting old?' she added, her voice stiffening like a manipulated nipple. The very voice which made 'In Bed with Madonna' such a frightening performance. Kylie tried to protest, but Madonna would have none of it.

'Oh shut it pussy woman,' Madonna said, reaching into her silk Gaultier trousers and pulling out a penis. 'This is when you get fucking lucky.' With that, Madonna forced her dripping cock down Kylie's throat.

Questioner: Did your parents abuse you as a child?

Narrator: Not while I was awake.

Questioner: But this Madonna & Kylie thing. It seems that all the women on the Heath are actually men. Are you a misogynist?

Narrator: No. The Heath is an escape from reality; a leap into truth.

Questioner: You've also written about Carla. She seems to be another dubious woman character on the Heath.

Narrator: Carla was a drag queen, not a woman. And she, like Madonna, was loved by men.

Questioner: Read out what you have written about her in your diary.

Narrator: Carla had severed her own hand and in its place was a rotating dildo. She used it to fuck people and then she killed them.

'Christ, what is zis place?' she would hiss. Carla had cocaine-coloured hair marooned on top of a daily-waxed face, eyebrows arched like bull whips and sticky lips that glistened like flypaper. Nightly, between her lips she trapped fat-bodied, skinny-legged flies. Once they'd gorged on her insides, they vomited over her—somewhat like the men she fucked.

Questioner: Why was she on the Heath?

Narrator: Carla wanted to be an actress. The Heath was the theatre hall she was never invited to perform at. No one pissed on her fire there, though many urinated on her.

Questioner: Is she truth or invention?

Narrator: She was a monstrous cartoon character. She graced the pages of an underground magazine, which has since been banned. A cult figure; a camp and pulpy stereotype for gay men to love. When the police handcuffed the publishers and banished her from print, Carla came to live on our homeland. She loved to stalk into the trees of the Heath and talk to a captivated crowd. She let some of them fist her. They usually didn't survive the night.

Questioner: But who would Carla appeal to?

Narrator: To one half of the gay psyche. The queer identity, so one theory runs, which splits rather helpfully between those who love hairdressing, cake baking and vanilla sex and those viscera loving sex monsters.

Questioner: Are you Carla?

Narrator: Carla is a metaphor for all the hard-faced drag queens who stretch their cocks tightly over their bollocks and up between the crack of their bony arses. Drag queens with square faces and angry eyes. Men who aren't quite beautiful and who aren't quite handsome. Now I'm not saying they're all like this. Some are beautiful. Anything is acceptable in gay life which is beautiful and uninfected.

Questioner: What did Carla do for you?

Narrator: She raped and pillaged gay stereotypes for me. My friends carried her with us into the nightclubs. 'Christ, what is zis place?' we would hiss as we weaved across the floor of venues such as the Market Tavern.

Questioner: What is the Market Tavern?

Narrator: At best, it is like a cold store; at worst, it's a nightclub. The air is pregnant with amyl nitrate. Dry ice billows in sinuous, art nouveau lines. Jaundiced youths undulate their hips to techno. The puce walls are lined with slabs of rotting meat. These burgundy-faced men want to be unhooked from old age so that they can perform congress with chickens. Boys who will lick the sweat off their still-breathing carcasses. The Market is like a Heath with the added attractions of a disco and a licensed bar.

Questioner: What did you do at this Heath with a disco?

Narrator: We created a self-enclosed world. We entertained each other with tales of murder and violence while others stamped bullets of spit into puddles of beer. We thought if we wrote down these tales we could sell them.

Questioner: Tell me about one of these fantasy tales you shared with your friends. I think it could be important.

Narrator: Well, I'm embarrassed to say because I know it's silly.

Questioner: But go on.

Narrator: Carla, on her way up to the Heath, would pick up one of the free magazines distributed outside tube stations which, as a fledgling journalist, I wrote docile fashion pieces for. In our fantasy Carla killed the editor, cut off the editor's face, and attached it to her own face with her modish 'babe' hair clips. She actually looked quite pretty for once. 'I'm zee editor now, lets do a piece about cruising on the Heath,' she would say. She'd sit at the computer unable to type because of the cherry nails jutting from her manly fingers. Carla was a fantastical invention and yet a channel for truth; a conduit for all our sulphurous, callous thoughts.

Questioner: Where did those dark thoughts come from?

Narrator: From the violent side of gay life?

Questioner: Which violence?

Narrator: Death from AIDS related illnesses perhaps. Or drugs.

Questioner: So is AIDS truth for you, or just a game?

Narrator: Both.

Questioner: Doesn't it worry you that you might be a deeply unpleasant character?

Narrator: Yes.

Questioner: And the Heath provides an escape from your unpleasant lives?

Narrator: No, the Heath is a chance to embrace them. On the Heath you jump from the emptiness of your life to the fullness of a horny fundament.

Questioner: Isn't there something frightening about that?

Narrator: Yes. And there's real danger too. One night, in bizarre circumstances, a man was hanged from a tree.

Questioner: Aren't you at all petrified by this? Or is this the ultimate goal of the Heath dweller? Ultimate destruction?

Narrator: Sometimes the dark dog crosses your path, sucks you off then spits your dismembered prick onto the floor. You shiver for a moment. Thoughts of death spear any calm. But the scary nights on the Heath are the best, more compelling than a perfectly lit Mapplethorpe and more appetising than foie gras.

And, by the way, serial killers like Colin Ireland have better things to do than root around in a piss-smeared landscape. They prefer clubs and a live P.A. to enjoy free of charge before the killing begins.

Questioner: Do you think of your mother when you're scared on the Heath?

Narrator: When in danger, I fantasise about the *TV Quick* story that will appear after my demise. The dodgy polaroids of my dear mother surrounded by cerise furnishing fabrics and holding a lavender embroidered handkerchief supplied by the magazine. 'Bearing up after the loss of her gay son,' the caption would read.

Questioner: And do you think of your Dad as well?

Narrator: Only when I'm fucking someone's arse off.

Questioner: What frightens you the most? Is there anything in the diary?

Narrator: Yes, and it reads as

follows:

There is a wizened guy who wears nothing but a jockstrap. He wanders over to me and grabs my arm like a child abuser to a blond 5 year old. In a slit of shitty light his face appears: old, mad, haunted and dangerous. The moustache which has assured tenancy beneath his nose glistens. His irridescent chest is slick with the ooze of piss and saliva, his torso bony like the mental patients who used to come into the staff bedroom looking for biscuits when I was a careworker.

I allow images of bias cut shifts and Madonna to sashay into my mind and blot him out. My eyes drop to his distended cock, covered with precum and someone else's shit. He says he wants to fuck my sweet little arse. He's pathetic, sad, infected. Angry, threatening and indestructible. He needs to be hit and told what a fuck he is. He has to be told he looks like a fucking drug addict staggering about the scrubland.

But these thoughts, which snake their way from mind to fist, are inspired by fear. I lash them off before the poison projects.

Questioner: Why do you stop?

Narrator: Because of truth: I see myself reflected in a shard of mirrored glass as it slices the top off my finger.

Questioner: And how does that make you feel?

Narrator: Like a watery shit slipping painfully from that tired arse.

Questioner: Does the Heath become more frightening than this as the night draws on?

Narrator: 5am on Hampstead Heath is the worst. Fear allows you to transcend yourself and become someone else. Let me read you this: **It was a dead night, brought alive only by an occasional slapping of calloused hand upon sagging arse followed by an appreciative whimper. This experience cauterised every nerve ending, including those in your arsehole.**

Out there was a stereotype called Tim who wanted a novice.

Tim had wide shoulders, which, were it not for medical intervention, might have killed his mother during childbirth. He was a viscera loving sex monster who, in a previous period, had enjoyed cakebaking with his mother and vanilla sex with his father. As a child, he'd regularly slipped his fingers up his arse and now he selflessly offered them to others. A hard man cliché, he wore camouflage trousers, a green bomber and a bare bulging torso where a tee shirt should have been. He was, I speak intuitively, quite afraid of what he really was:

'I hate sad poofs.'

Instead of being one, he terrorized those he met. He knew abuse alone was what could separate him from the prissy cocksuckers he nightly terrorized. Or in his mind at least.

'Yeah you fucking love it,' he would rant, bucking his fatty meat into someone's face.

Questioner: What did the other men get from this?

Narrator: In the larder of their minds was a shelf marked 'danger'.

They were only happy when it was full. For some, that meant a humiliating moment with Tirn. It reminded them of the school bully.

'Last night I saw a pretty guy of about 18 being kicked to shit over there,' Tim said, pointing into the sooty emptiness. 'The worse part was that it wasn't being done properly.'

'It's criminal Tim,' I could hear Madonna saying in my head.

'So I got involved, did it right, got him to suck me,' he recounted.

'Amazing Tim,' said Carla in my head, 'do you have an address card?'

'Yeah you're my type,' he went on. 'Are you a top? Because we can turn some guys over up here together then go home and give them a good sorting out.'

'Sounds a dream, Prince,' I said.

'Don't act camp, it doesn't suit you,' he told me, 'In nine months you won't recognize yourself. I've got skinhead friends you know.'

Then he grabbed my balls (or were they someone else's?) and wrenched them, trying with his other hand to stick three fingers up a vacant arse. He was sliding into the earth which itself was spurting from every orifice a slurry of piss and shit. His hand was a vice, his mouth a spitting machine.

Questioner: Is this real or did it happen in your mind?

Narrator: No, it happened by the Deer Park.

Listen to this:

Tim pushed the guy's sad head down to his boots. 'Yeah fucking suck it' he shouted in the way fading porn stars do, spitting at him over and over again. A special needs client I used to work with used to spit at me with that kind of hatred; it was similarly unpleasant and equally contrived.

The hard teeth of the cocksucker was now slicing off maybe two layers of skin. Tim leered at me and to himself, even.

'Yeah it feels fucking ace Tim,' I lied, forcing myself further into the cocksuckers mouth. Now it had become like a scene Verlaine might have loved.

Questioner: So what did you learn from Tim?

Narrator: That sex is truth. And that little else is. If I let the hand that strokes me twist full up inside my arse, I could probably understand more. I am Tim; but at other times I want to be Madonna or Carla. These are all characters through which a gay identity can flow. But when the queer identity splits down the middle, you have to decide which side you want to bat for.

Still life with an idea of a
trailer park
Jay Merill

Summer in the trailer park. All blare-and-glare.
Sweaty, dusty, rusty. Sex, drugs, rock'n'roll. Ultimate
tv road movie. Red and yellow food on paper plates.
Dry-cracked peeling formica. And the trailer park in
tinny winter. Snow covered car wreckage in mounds,
iced over trailers. Silver strip, blackened at the edges,
hanging sideways from the last remaining nails.
Frozen, bleak. She had her trailer park fantasies.

*A round orange pumpkin
with yellow flecks and
neat creases. Full
and sleek with its
mottled stalk
protruding.
Dense, weighty,
vegetable-cool.
Fresh-leather
skin, smooth
textured. She
runs a finger down
the line of a
pumpkin crease.*

Queen of the trailer park. Nylon leopardskin. Lying posily in her trailer. A plastic woodgrain environment. Surfaces edged in gold metallic strip embossed with figurines. Reclining in her trailer of ivory white and chrome. Red polished toenails. Her feet held in points like a dancer's. Rattle of a radio. Romantic-corny tune. She sways, mouths sentimental phrases from a 1950s ballad.

Six o'clock in the evening at Charing Cross. Yellow lights, smell of vanilla sugar, smell of coffee. Everybody hurrying. The nice-cold winter of stations that is pleasing and not so frightening as trailerparks. A woman, carrying a pumpkin, meets a man by the coffee stall. They smile, they dance around one another, the pumpkin glowing between them. Soft orange.

Turquoisy bright blanket. A fitted gas fridge under a false drawer with the grain going crossways. A sink with a plug as tiny as a fingertip and a table that folds into a bed. All this, the essence of a trailer.

Carrying the pumpkin, turning it around in both hands. Too beautiful to be hidden away in a bag.
—It's a present. I've brought it for you as a present.
—A giant worry bead, he says.
She holds her hands still, steadying the pumpkin, turns away from him.
—All you need now is a fairy godmother.

He laughs. They walk a few paces. She cannot look
at his face. He asks if she is thinking of being herself
a fairy godmother. She makes a rapid gasp meaning
'Not.' She stares at a pinstripe section of his leg.

A *fairy godmother* is a worker of magic and as such
is powerful, but is never the main protagonist and has
the soul of a midwife. This is not the right model for
the woman in the trailer.

His fast changing smile. Sunny-cloudy, flash of
mistrust, now serene.
—What am I meant to do with it?
—If the pumpkin embarrasses you, bury it in the
garden. Then you won't have to see it. (Her voice
slightly barbed.) Suddenly, unexpectedly, she looks into
his face. World spins, heads rock, eyes lock. The
lighted noisy station fades away.

Red and yellow backdrop. Strident Mexicana.
Blanket with splodges of turquoise and black. Painted-
pointed toes resting on scatter cushions. Blue, orange,
mauve. Pearly frostpink lips, smile. 5 waxy roses with
peagreen leaves in a silver vase perched on a knick-
knackery shelf. Shrinal white light pours from a fluted
lamp. Through the window the dark-night sky.

Patches of dazzling light, smell of coffee. Warm-
wrapped figures pass. A man and a woman,

eyelocked, lean on the shadowed side of a coffee stall.
—Did you give me the pumpkin because it's Halloween?
That's why, is it? Should I cook it or keep it?
They walk from the shadows onto the bright concourse.
Everyone very kind-in-the-eyes seeing the woman carrying
the pumpkin. She wonders if she is doing it to see kind
eyes.
—You could scoop out the pulp and make a lantern head.
You could roast the seeds.
She hands the pumpkin to the man. He strokes the dark
orange-yellow flecked pumpkin skin.
—We could talk about the symbols, he
is saying.
—Yes. The pumpkin
possibilities.
They move towards the
trains, arms linked, feeling
body-heat through coat
sleeves.

Outside in the tinny winter
night a bare branch, shaken
by the wind, taps against a
door panel. The queen of the
trailer park hears the click, click,
against the squirls of frosted glass. She smooths her spiky
yellow hair and lowers her eyelids, gives a nylon
leopardskin smile. Husky, golden oldie always. 'Are you
lonesome tonight?'

TEUTONIC PLATES

Mark Love

"Go on then...ask me," said the stick insect
in the torn shellsuit. Beside him the woman
scowled a little, then a little more as her
companion dug a skinny elbow into the
greasy folds of her padded jacket.
"Gracie," she stated vehemently before
spitting down between her toeless
Reeboks.

Behind them on the side-chapel steps a mound
of blackened tweed quivered corpulently and
mumbled something that sounded like "Cabbage."
The Stick Insect was delighted.
"Earthquakes? I'll tell you about earthquakes
if you like. I know all about earthquakes
cos I went to school...not like some," he
frowned, jabbing a horny thumbnail back
towards the fortress of musty tweed and
its moat of wind-goosed carrier bags.

"There are some as of never opened a book less it were to blow their nose into," said Stick Insect haughtily. "Others of us, of course, own books for themselves...I have a green one."

Suddenly the woman beside him seemed taken by a great sadness and began to cry vigorously. There were two permanent trails through the dirt down the lumpen putty of her face which glistened now — shiny streams of glacial misery. Stick Insect watched fascinated as the stream flowed from the small glassy eyes down the plump, vein webbed cheeks to a jump-off point on her cheek and into the compilation of fleshy excesses below.

In a fit of compassion, Stick Insect threw his arms around her and pulled her close — holding her tight despite her struggling until he spied the long outflow of mucus being breathed in and out from the sooty nostrils to the cracked, flaking lips.

"Yer bastard," he screamed, tottering on wrist-thin legs and holding onto the baggy crotch of the shellsuit where a hidden can sloshed warmly. "Yer dirt," he yelled again, slapping at the woman's shoulder with his free hand.

The woman gasped for breath between bawls, shaking the trail of mucus somewhere behind her. "Gracie," she cried once more and then crumpled down into her usual inertia. From behind her came a snort and an utterance that just might have been "Cabbage."

"Earthquakes?" said the Stick Insect delightedly. "I know all about earthquakes." He sat where he'd stood, disturbing a cheesy polystyrene Big Mac box with the can in his crotch. "Y'see earthquakes is caused by these

big, huge...massive plates that countries sit on. And
these teutonic plates go CRASH," — he illustrated with
surprising vigour, ramming his fist into the polystyrene
loud enough to solicit an outraged "Cabbage" growl from
the mound behind and a faint blubbering from the woman
beside him. A steady flow of liquid begAn to bubble
through the tiny rips in the crotch of the shellsuit
and flow down the church steps toward the street.

"And...disasters happen," he sighed, his deep-set,
sorrowful eyes catching the movement of ants washed
away in the slackening flow of the lager leaking from
his shellsuit. "Oh."

The woman began to giggle to herself. She batted a
bashful eye in his direction then threw her arms around
his neck and kissed him hard.

Stick Insect embraced her back, first squeezing tight
about her shoulders then each breast in turn, then the
rolls of flesh that burst past the safety-pinned front
of the jacket until he found what he was looking for.
The woman grinned her yellowed grin, delighted, and
pinched her eyelids together, not noticing the sly
theft of the half-empty brandy miniature.

A push made her rock away from him and sit nodding
happily. He glanced at the crucified Christ hanging
from the wall and hurriedly crossed himself. Then he
turned away slightly and, despite his wrist's incessant
shaking, added the meagre contents of the bottle to the
stale leavings in the can held between his legs.

"Cabbage," snorted the mound.

Stick Insect's eyes widened in delight. "Earthquakes?
I know all about earthquakes. Y'see earthquakes is
caused by these massive, big plates that countries sit
on and these big teutonic plates go CRASH!" He jumped
up from his step and slapped together his bony hands as
hard as he could, startling a pigeon enough to further

foul the hanging Christ.

 A tear began to form in the woman's eye before the last feather had fallen to earth, while behind them both the Mound grumbled in his sleep and emitted a long, hissing fart.

 The Stick Insect stood quite still as the little river of pleasant smelling liquid escaped the upturned can between his knees. "And then..." he sighed, watching the ants swirl over the steps towards the pavement, "...disasters happen."

the promise of
Sweet Things

jemma kennedy

LURED BY THE PROMISE OF SWEET THINGS, **I am taken out one hot Saturday by my friend Michelle and her father to visit two other little girls, daughters of Michelle's Auntie Holly.**

"They always let us have chocolate milk at Jane's house," Michelle reminds me as we climb inside her father's car, and I imagine it dreamily, pale and chalky-smooth, the seduction of forbidden confectionery. I am nearly six, I think, and in time I will be able to buy my own sweets, but not yet. Treats are few in my house as my mother distrusts chocolate.

I have heard a lot about Michelle's friends and the mountains of sweets they consume. Already they are a fixture in my head, a source of envy which I play with like an unhealed cut. What Michelle has and what I lack forms the slack of our friendship; a skipping-rope, now loose, now pulled taut between us. But sometimes I am permitted to share in Michelle's spoils, like today. We will play with the girls, we will be given sweets by the grown-ups. These coming pleasures loom over me, making me anxious, heavy with the weight of anticipation.

WE DRIVE THROUGH QUIET WEEKEND STREETS **to a distant suburb. I gaze out of the window at row upon row of identical houses. There is little to break up the landscape**—a child's pram abandoned on its side in the road, a dog that lolls in the sun, panting, flanks twitching as if stung by an invisible whip. My throat is dry, I think of swimming-pools, of ice-cream. It is midday, windless and bright. The occasional screams of playing children smack on and off the baking tarmac.

I can see Michelle's father in the wing mirror, arm hanging out of the window, cigarette in the hand that holds the steering wheel. I am supposed to call him Uncle Jack, but can barely bring myself to, as he doesn't look like an uncle. My two real uncles have long hair and roll their own cigarettes, let me lick the gummed strip on their rolling papers, give me sticks of chewing gum. Jack wears mirrored sunglasses and hums along to the radio, ignoring Michelle and me fidgeting on the hot back seat. Friends of Michelle's sister Suzanne, who is thirteen, say Jack looks just like the pop-singer they are all in love with. Jack is big, with thick sandy hair on his head, his arms, the backs of his hands. Pale blue eyes match his jeans and denim jacket.

Finally, Jack pulls into a carpark in front of a huge white building, with dark shingles covering its upper half. Big letters spell out a name on the roof. I know one of the words, 'Hotel', but not the other one. I am puzzled, wondering where the little girls' house is, thinking this can't be it. Jack locks the car, takes us both by the hand and leads us towards the double doors which stand open. His hand is rough and I trot to keep up with his long steps, watching his feet in their scuffed deck shoes like the ones we wear for PE. The rubber soles make a dull bouncing sound on the ground. We find ourselves in a long room with a high counter running the length of the wall, which is covered with hundreds of bottles. It is cool and dark in here and the air smells sticky, like lemonade. A few men are gathered in the corner watching football on the TV screen. They hug their glasses to their chests and blow smoke at the ceiling, murmuring to each other. At the other end of the bar, Jack lifts Michelle and me on to high stools and we perch there, giggling. Michelle's Auntie Holly is behind the bar, fluffy yellow jumper stretched tightly across her chest, but she doesn't look hot. She leans across and smiles at us.

"Hello sweethearts," she says, pulling up a section of the polished counter like a trapdoor and coming out. She kisses Michelle and then Jack, quickly, and laughs, winking at me. I smile back at her carefully, wanting to please her, privately admiring her name and her yellow sweater.

Michelle says, "Can we have cherries, Auntie Holly?"

"Please," says Jack.

"Please," Michelle says, and Holly laughs and reaches over the bar. She hands us both a cocktail cherry speared on a stick. The cherries are red, glossy, perfectly round, and the sweetness lingers on my tongue.

"Now then," Holly says, "The girls are waiting for you upstairs. Jack, can you take them up?"

Jack nods and we scramble off our stools and follow him across the room, through swing doors and up a red-carpeted staircase. I am excited by now at the size and strangeness of all this, full of questions which I'm not quite sure of, and don't want to ask Jack. Thinking about it, I realise that I am scared of Jack. This secret knowledge pleases me, as it is something I can't share with Michelle.

Upstairs, Jack opens a door at the end of a long corridor. He pokes his head around it and then motions us through. I hang back, waiting for Michelle to go in first, and then walk through, keeping close behind her.

"Stay here and play," Jack says, looking at us sternly. "No messing, all right?" and he shuts the door behind us.

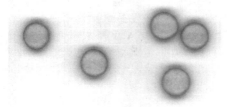

AFTER THE SUNLIT HALLWAY, the room we are in is gloomy. Thick rose-coloured curtains pulled across the window shut out most of the light—a single ray of sun slants through the fabric. When my eyes adjust I see that everything in the room: bedspreads, carpet, lampshades, wallpaper—is pink and shabby like a damp flannel. The cool air smells stale and yet sweet, like perfume. Two girls, both a little bigger than me, sit in the middle of the floor, dressing dolls. They look up at us unsmilingly. Both of them have long tangled brown hair and are wearing dirty white socks. Michelle skips towards them and sings, "Hello Jane, hello Jennifer, hello, hello, hello, hello." The smaller of the sisters giggles once and then turns back to her doll, slowly buttoning up a tiny cardigan. Michelle marches around the room touching things to demonstrate her familiarity with this place, her possession of the girls, who continue to ignore us, intent on their activity. I sit cross-legged on the floor by the window and wait for someone to speak to me. A row of broken glass shards from a chandelier hangs from the curtain-rail on pieces of string. One piece manages to catch the sunlight, casting a rainbow chip on the carpet. I touch the warm patch of light with my finger, and hear a motorbike roar down the street outside. The noise of the bike, the sunshine beyond these walls feel unreachable. I hear the sisters whispering. I try to judge how long a minute is, but lose count before I get to sixty.

Suddenly, as if triggered by a silent playtime bell, Jane and Jennifer put their dolls down and leap to their feet. They begin to race around the room playing tag. Michelle joins in instantly, so I stand up and begin to chase her, and before long all four of us are screaming with delight and jumping up and down on the beds, pushing and tagging each other randomly. In between bounces the sisters throw questions at me; what's my name, how old am I, where do I live, where's my school, am I Michelle's best friend? I pant out my answers, as I know, copying them, that I'm not supposed to stop moving while I speak. I also know that the last question is a dangerous one, and am thinking of the best way to reply when Michelle tugs my hair hard, as if answering for me. The pain jerks into my excitement, blurring my vision, and I pause and think about crying, but the moment passes and I keep running, careful not to get left behind in the game. I feel as if we have been in this room for hours, as if I have known the girls for ever. But the game is over—Jennifer, the older sister, is bored with it and flops down on the floor. We copy her immediately and lie on our stomachs, catching our breath.

Now that we are friends, the sisters show us some of their treasures: a white satin stiletto shoe, a soda-siphon, some lipsticks in gilt cases, a photograph of a puppy dressed up in baby clothes, a pair of nylon panties with a picture of a man printed on them.

"It's Elvis Presley," Jane points out. I don't know who Elvis Presley is, but I know by the way she says this that the panties are something quite special so I stare at them very hard. Michelle demands to play with the makeup. Jennifer paints a thick grainy line of lipstick on Michelle's mouth, on Jane's mouth. Then it is my turn. I purse my lips as I have seen the others do while Jennifer cakes them with lipstick. It feels waxy, heavy on my face. After a minute I wipe most of it off with the back of my hand. Michelle and Jane squirt each other with jets of water from the soda-siphon and squeal.

"Stop that, you two," Jennifer orders. "Now I'll show you a thing." She lifts up one of the twin mattresses, pulls out some magazines and spreads them on the floor. We crowd around on hands and knees while Jennifer turns the pages. Colour photographs of women, sitting with their legs wide apart. They aren't wearing any clothes but they are wearing a lot of makeup. Michelle touches her mouth, still stained red with lipstick, and says nothing. Jennifer wears a bored expression but glances at us to make sure we are looking.

"These are Daddy's comics," Jane says proudly, stroking the glossy pages with her hand. I gaze at the photographs—bewildered by the women and their poses but strangely excited by the way they touch themselves so possessively, the way they look up at me through lowered lashes, holding parts of their bodies as if offering them up for me to touch.

"That lady looks like Auntie Holly," Michelle says, giggling, pointing at a woman with dark hair and shining, oiled skin. The woman's face is a little like Auntie Holly's, but Jennifer snatches the magazine away from Michelle and says, "No she doesn't, stupid. My Mum's a lot prettier than that, anyway. Prettier than your Mum."

"She isn't," Michelle says furiously, pinching Jane, who is sitting nearer to her. Jane begins to cry. Jennifer kicks Michelle's foot and Michelle starts wailing and turns away from us towards the wall. The sisters crawl into another part of the room and find their dolls. I slip out of the door.

OUTSIDE THE GIRLS' ROOM IT IS SUNNY AND VERY QUIET . I walk back down the corridor towards the staircase. There are closed doors on either side. I count six doors before I reach the stairs and stop in front of the last door on the left—noises are coming from inside, high on the sleepy air, a woman crying. I wait and listen. From some unknown place I find a response within me to the rise and fall of the cries and their surrounding silence—something familiar and yet far away, like the hot summer afternoon outside this big house. I push the door open gently and step inside. The woman's voice swells around me, and I hear another deeper voice below it. I stand just in front of the door and look at the two people who are in the room with me, lying on the bed. Although I can hear her, I can't see the woman very well, only her bare, open knees and her hair—it is the man I look at, his nakedness, his size. His face is obscured.

I glance around the room which is huge and almost empty except for the large bed and a dressing-table with a mirror over which clothes are hanging. I can see stockings, a white slip. On the far wall the window is open wide. Half-drawn curtains swell in the breeze; a shaft of sunlight catches hundreds of spinning dust motes on their path through the air. On the bed the couple are joined in a slow movement, pulled together by the sounds they are making. Their noises occupy the room fully. The bed creaks, the man's shoulders stretch and elongate, shiny with sweat, the backs of his legs and buttocks strain towards something I can't be sure of. His head is buried in the woman's neck; her hair is spread over the pillow in dark waves but her face is twisted away, towards the wall. Her feet are pointed towards me, the toenails painted cherry-red. With my eyes I measure the space between the locked figures and the high ceiling with its plaster flowers melting into the corners where it meets the walls. I am unsurprised by it all, caught up in the almost-quiet of the afternoon, the noises riding on its back, the sunlight and shade dancing on the walls. I am held, suspended in the couple's abandonment, their obliviousness to my presence; the closeness, the privacy of their act.

The woman's cries are high, delicate, evenly pitched. The man moans deep from the back of his throat and then his back rears up. Instinctively I duck and crouch down by the floor next to the bed. A pair of navy deck shoes lie on the carpet, near my hand. My heart is thumping.

Can I see myself here, in a room like this, flung into a distant future, covered completely by a pair of legs and a back as strong and solid as wood, my fingers clutching and slipping off its surface? Perhaps the promise of sensation, the sweetness of touch, of taste, of smell, is already there in my small arms and legs, my hands and feet, my face which I have known forever, my body which feels infinitely malleable, like plasticine, and which does anything I tell it to. I wrap my arms around myself and kneel on the carpet, as still as can be. The room is quiet except for the sound of breathing. The man and woman breathe together, deeply and evenly, and I regulate my breathing to match theirs. The three of us inhale and exhale and I am drifting towards sleep when the man grunts, waking me. I get on to my hands and knees and crawl towards the door. I stand up without looking back at the bed, although I want to, and open the door enough to squeeze through. The man says, "What?" in a thick, sleepy voice. The latch clicks softly behind me and I carry his question with me, back down the corridor.

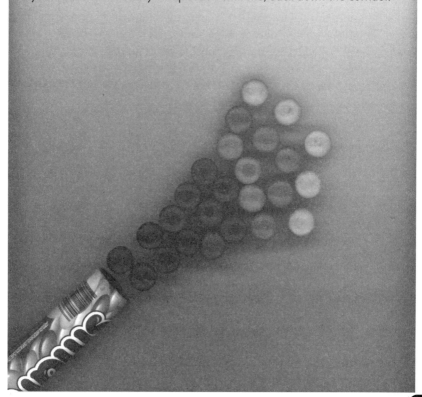

IN THE GIRLS' BEDROOM THE THREE OF THEM SIT IN A CIRCLE, each brushing the hair of the one in front. Lost in the importance of their task, none of them notice me come in, so I sit on the end of one of the beds, which sags beneath me, and watch. I wonder if I am invisible. Minutes pass and I daydream —it could be ten or twenty minutes before Jack comes into the bedroom and says, "Hey there," throwing each of us a small carton. Jane and Jennifer cheer and Michelle looks at me triumphantly. I look at it. Chocolate milk. I say, "Thank you Uncle Jack," and hold the carton in my hand. It is running with beads of icy water which have soaked through my dress where it landed in my lap. It seems impenetrable, but by copying the others I manage to pierce the silver hole on top of the carton with the straw gummed to the side. I pull the sweet liquid into my mouth, so cold it makes my throat ache. This moment should be significant, as I have waited for it all afternoon. There is pleasure in the taste, certainly, but it is outweighed by the pictures in my head, as tangled as the girls' hair before they began their brushing. Jane, Jennifer and Michelle suck on their straws, still seated in a triangle. Jennifer has braided Michelle's hair into messy plaits which are tied together with bits of pink string. Jack stands in the middle of the room, staring down at the naked women left forgotten, posturing on the carpet. He glances up and I catch his eye. He opens his mouth as if to speak, but then closes it, slapping a tube of Smarties against his denim thigh like a baton, in a slow, steady rhythm. Suddenly he tosses the tube to me with a flick of his wrist, and it lands on the floor by my feet. I pick the sweets up.

"Look at my hair, Daddy," Michelle says coquettishly. I think of Auntie Holly, I don't know why.

"Finish your game," Jack says, "It's time to leave."

LATER, ON THE WAY HOME IN THE CAR, NOTHING SEEMS TO HAVE CHANGED VERY MUCH. The sun has gone in and Jack is silent behind his sunglasses. Michelle is tired and complains, whining for more sweets. The memory of chocolate is in my mouth. I feel ancient, exhausted by the distances I have travelled. For me, discoveries are frequent at the moment—words, secrets, the taste of forbidden sugar on my tongue—sensations as new as milk which I want to store up somewhere they can't be touched, grasping them like a kite-string before they slip out of my hand, up out of reach.

COME ON YOU BLUES

by
Ralph
Dartford

8:30am. The alarm clock triggers its quadraphonic jangle, ricochets off the walls and splices into my brain like a swarm of hot bullets. It remains there until 9:17 when a shit, shower and shave pull them clean. At 9:26 I slug a jug of black coffee, no breakfast. I've got to be hungry and lean. Eating later will cut conversation. From 10:02 a cunning mood invades me as I renew a deep friendship with clothing unworn since the last conflict. I decide on the lime green suit. At 10:46 I commence smoking and pacing. I run my tongue over an infected tooth. It creates a numbing white noise in my forehead. I flick on the radio to divert my attention, journey through the wavebands and land on the news station. America is going to wipe Haiti off its windscreen. The time now is 11:33. I am tense. I am taut.

I have a toothache. I've gone through half a pack of Silk Cut. The ashtray is overflowing. She is late.

11:58. A knock at the door.
"Hello big brother."
"You're late little sister."
"Yeah didn't know what to wear. You look like Paul Gascoigne."
"Fuck off! You look like Anneka Rice."
"No you fuck off."
"Are we going or what?"

It's 12:05. My sister Avrail is driving. Driving fast. I'm strapped to the driving seat, chewing gum and stroking terror. We have not spoken since she put the key in the ignition. I don't think we are going to. What's new.
"I never thought it would happen to me and a girl from Clapham."
"Up the junction, Squeeze," Avrail is answering, "It's all

so easy."
"You're right and always easy."
I've broken the ice, traditions are there I suppose.
"Your turn." I'm warming.
"And it's got to be a London band."
I'm gazing out of the window at the useless countryside and poising myself for the obscure. Avrail drives over a dead fox. Finally: "With a trill in my heart and a pill on my tongue, dissolve the nerves that have just begun."
"True, Spandau Ballet," I'm shouting.
"There's a good boy."
We're playing the lyric game. The game we've played for years, ever since the television exploded half way through Coronation Street. It used to be simple, songs from the top thirty, teen fodder. As we grew older we became more selective. It got tougher until it got ridiculous. Bands on certain labels, towns and attitudes.
I remember the night when it got personal. It was the last time we played.

We were drunk in a pub with friends neither of us see any more. Throughout the evening they had tried to play with us, but soon dropped out. They were out of their depth, strictly Sunday league players. We pissed all over them.
"I heard you let that little friend of mine take off your party dress," Avrail said with a cocky slur.
"Allison, Elvis Costello." I replied dribbling. "But it don't count cos' Elvis don't wear glasses."
"What do you fuckin' mean Elvis don't wear glasses?" Avrail thrust a copy of that week's NME in my face with a bespectacled Elvis adorning the cover. I hated her smelly friend from Glasgow who'd pulled it from his Donald Duck duffel bag.

"Yeah he wears glasses, but it's not legit' 'cos he wears em as a pose. He can see just as well as you and me."
"You're as blind as a fuckin' bat!"
"He does! He also wears em as a psychological barrier so he doesn't have to confront his audience."
"Bollocks you wanker!"
The table went berserk when she poured her untouched pint of snakebite over my head.
A week later in the same pub amongst some friends, Avrail hauled out a cassette player from a Co-Op carrier bag.
"Everyone shut up. My brother Mr Magoo, your time is up."
She pressed play. A recorded telephone conversation between her and a representative of Elvis Costello's record company confirmed that our man was indeed short sighted. She'd won.

`12:18.` The silence has returned. Avrail lights a Rothmans which breaks it. She's singing along to 'War' by Edwin Starr. It cannons out of the car stereo and rattles me.
My sister can't sing for toffee. Neither can I.

`12:20.` My melancholy is getting the better of me.
I was nine years old. Avrail was almost eight. I remember rocking her in a chair by the french windows. A summer storm approaching. Our parents arguing. I sang her songs I'd made up. I tried to rock her to sleep but all she did was wail.

`12:26.` I'm sweating.
"We're almost here, pass me a mint," Avrail orders.
I'm reaching for the dashboard and struggling with the G-force. "I can't cope with this," I say, turning to her. I'm panicking.
"I know you can't, but for once will you just compromise? If you get stroppy like last year I'll fuckin' kill you. Mum still hasn't got over it, she's been slurping sherry since breakfast."
"I don't give a toss about Mum. Is he coming?"
"No he's in Leeds, poor bastard, fuckin' terrified to step outside his front door."
"I didn't mean to butt him."
"Yeah right."
"Just that he called Dad old."
"Well he is isn't he?"
"But he fuckin' laughed as he said it, why did he have to laugh?"
"For fuck's sake shut up, it's Grandma's 80th birthday."
Grandma's birthday. The annual gathering of the clan. I hate most of these people, their meddling, their lack of respect. Their curdling cash equals a Corfu taxi driver mentality.
Fuck em'!

I'm having a mint as well, something to dissolve the nerves that have just begun. My toothache isn't getting better.

I'm looking across at my sister. The sun is shining now, slanting across her face giving her the look of a cool heroine. I want to tell her that I love her. I want to tell her she is beautiful.

Can't, it's not the family way. It's an autumn Sunday.

12:32. Half an hour late. Grandma sits between two empty chairs, already an afterthought. Like an apology, an unopened bottle of champagne stands in front of her. Those chairs either side of her will remain empty.

They're all here, my sister, aunts, uncles and cousins,

minus one. Mum who is pissed. Dad who is lost. I'm shaking hands and patting backs, kissing and cuddling. They will not look me in the eye.

We are sitting at a long pine table in this theme restaurant called The Anvil. There are ancient farm tools positioned everywhere. Avrail is to my right. A collection of brass spades to my left. I can't escape. Maybe I can dig myself out.

We're eating what is boasted on the menu as the best meat in Essex. It's good. Good enough for dogs. I'll eat fuckin' floorboards. Anything to save me from discussing the worrying growth of Pakistani newsagents with Aunt Lyn who sits opposite me in satin blue.

I'm chewing in time to the rhythm of the second hand of my wrist watch. Things are going well. I'll be home by 2:30. Home with the mass grave in the ash tray and the fresh ones already being dug in Haiti. But for the moment my head is down and I am eating spinach.

1:05. My toothache must be subsiding. I'm on my third helping of fat-injected beef. I've drunk five glasses of vile German wine.

I'm desperate for a piss. Everyone peers over their

plates as I make my way to the lavatory. I feel their sense of relief as I fade from view. I'm relieving myself in the long metallic urinal and playing sink the Belgrano with the floating fag-butts. I'm washing my hands and face. I can't recognise myself in the mirror. I'm looking for a towel to dry my hands. I'm rummaging in my jacket pockets for a hanky but I pull out a small square of folded paper.

It's speed, amphetamine sulphate, Billy Whizz! The glorious drug of my youth. How the fuck did it get into my jacket pocket? I haven't worn this suit for a year. It's been longer than that since I touched anything like this. It's my thirty first birthday next month.

What the fuck is going on? I used to take speed in my late teens. On Friday nights I bought it for a tenner a time

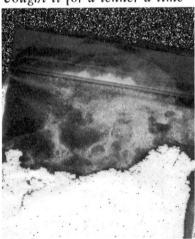

from Mick the Malt in Dean Street. Then I'd go dancing until dawn, talking bullshit and creating a new world, always ending in sweaty, smelly sex in strange beds. Good times.

One night I took too much. I was working as a stage manager in a theatre in the West-End. I went to work one Saturday afternoon after a wild night in Wardour Street and promptly collapsed. They put me in a cab and sent me to hospital. I told the driver to take me to the rail station instead. When I got home I rang my boss and told him it was just nervous exhaustion. On the doctor's instructions I should take a couple of days off. When I returned to work they sacked me. They'd phoned the hospital.

I loved that job.

I'm lurching in and out of the toilet cubicle like a spastic waiter.

Should I throw it down the pan or should I save it for later.

Fuck it! Swallow it now.

1:35. The meal is finished and we're in the bar. I'm like an excited fly. My mind is darting everywhere. I want to talk to everyone I really do. I'm smiling at relatives. They turn their backs.

I'm standing alone gasping for a drink. I'm fighting with the

change in my pocket.
"What are you having?" It's
Avrail with a crisp twenty.
"Pint of lager, thanks. You
still making a killing, then?"
"Getting by, getting by."
"What're you selling these

She walked me around for
hours. Over hills, through
fields and across shit sodden
fields. Every five minutes she'd
wink and say, "Almost there"
and sprint ahead. After about
three hours it was getting dark

days?"
"Not much, same sort of
thing."
"What sort of thing is that
then Avrail?"
She's walking over to where
Mum is standing. They
embrace. She gloats at me.
She's always been Mum's
favourite.
Avrail is bad to the bone. She
may have killed. She's rich,
having always dealt in the
dubious. I wonder if she had
anything to do with the speed.
I'm rubbing my tongue against
my tooth and swallowing hard.
I must look like a goldfish in
the throes of death.
Avrail and I have always had
a spiteful relationship.
Avrail knew a place where
there were tanks, planes and
guns. I believed her. We were
seven and six years old. She
said she would take me there,
to the secret field. She kept me
in suspense for weeks. One
pissing rainy day she took me.

and she turned around and
said, "There are no tanks. You
really believed me didn't you.
You are useless, fuckin'
useless."
She told her mates and for
days they teased me. "Have
you seen the planes yet, Mr
Useless."
I got my own back a few
weeks later, or at least I
thought I did. Avrail was
bewitched by Alvin Stardust
and had posters of him all
over her bedroom wall. I
flushed them down the toilet.
She broke my nose when she
found out.
Avrail returns, sporting a razor
grin.
"Are we going then?" I'm
asking her.
"In a bit. You feeling alright?"
"Yeah fine, got a toothache."
"Come and talk to Dad."
"Alright."
Dad is sitting next to
Grandma at the back of the
room away from everyone else.

He has a pint of pale ale in his hand. Grandma is just staring.

"Hello son, how's it going?"

"Fine, working hard, how about you?"

"Not so bad. The Blues did

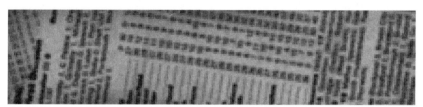

well yesterday."

"Yeah 2-0 win."

My Dad has just spoken of something that I thought died in his heart years ago. I'm almost overcome with grief. When I was young, Friday nights in the old house were the scenes of amazing tension. That was when the Blues played their home matches. They didn't play on Saturdays in those days because they had a market in their car park.

Dad would come home from work all filthy and ragged. He'd wash, change his clothes and eat his dinner. I'd hover around the kitchen and wait for his magic words. Dad knew the agony he was putting me through. Years later I realised he enjoyed it. Eventually he'd fold his paper up and push his plate away. He'd look around the room for what seemed forever and then say, "Let's go son." My coat was on and we were out the front door into the sodium night.

The journeys to the stadium were great. We had to get there by kickoff and Dad drove like a madman. He'd shout at other drivers who got in his way. "Fuck off you stupid cunt!" Once inside the stadium he'd buy me a meat pie and a can of tepid cola. The pies were always burnt. The game was important, but now I realise they were not as important as the two of us huddled together chanting "COME ON YOU BLUES." Through rain, snow and gale force winds we were always there. Avrail came a few times, but by then she was already playing much more devious games.

After the game Dad drove even faster. On the way home he'd stop at the local dog track, just in time for the last race. He'd get out of the car and vanish for about ten minutes. I'd be left alone with my bobble hat and my crumpled programme. When he returned he'd sometimes be laughing and sometimes swearing. One night he came back and he was crying. After that night we never went to see the Blues again.

Years later I wondered if he was interested in me, or was it just a sly way to gamble behind Mum's back.

I know now just by looking at him that he loved me, still does.

"Do you fancy coming to a game sometime Dad?"

"Yes. That will be nice son."

"Right, I'll sort it then."

We're smiling at each other. We have signed a treaty. Everything is dissolving. The years of confusion and non-communication and sometimes I think hate. I'm going to put my arms around him and tell him our new life begins here, from this very moment.

I love him and I'll going to tell him.

COME ON YOU BLUES

"Dad do you know that I..."

"Are you going to buy me a drink back or what, you tight bastard?"

"Yeah alright."

I'm going to tell him. I've got to tell him.

"You'll have to buy them Avrail. I haven't got enough."

"Always the poor fucker."

"I'll have a pint of lager."

"I'm proud of you big brother. You made a real effort today, talking to Dad. Are you going to have a word with Mum?"

"No I can't. I'm speeding out of my nut Avrail. I found it

in my jacket pocket. It helps me to talk to people, speed. It must have been a whole gram."

"You're what?"

"I found it in my jacket pocket, I don't know how it got there but I feel fuckin' great. I love Dad and I love you, give us a hug."

"You idiot. That was my speed. I borrowed that jacket when I was looking after your flat last year. Is there any left?"

"No I did the lot. Give us a hug. I love you. Give us a kiss."

"Fuck off you pervert, don't touch me. Fuck off."

I'm trying to put my arms around her but she's pushing me away. She is spitting at me.

There's a raised voice behind us. It's Dad. I've got to tell him.

"What are you two having a barney about then?"

"Nothing Dad, my big brother is just being a prat. Have you got that two hundred you owe me Dad?"

"I can't pay you back Avrail. I ain't got it. Maybe next month when I'm a little bit straight."

"It's always next fuckin' month with you Dad. I know you got the money, now fuckin' give it to me."

"I haven't got it love I, just haven't."

"Do you know what you are

Dad? A fuckin' loser."
The room has become silent,
slow motion and maybe sepia.
I'm lunging forward. Let me
tell him.
"Fuckin' leave him Avrail,"
I'm screaming. "I love you
Dad. I love you."
"Oh fuck me! The bigger loser
wants to have a go now does
he? Fuck off to your little
world of films and pop music
you streak of piss."
"Shut up you evil bastard.
Leave Dad alone. I love you
Dad."
"Why what are you going to
do? Butt me like your little
cousin last year. You're
nothing, big brother. You can't
even have kids. Oh yeah I
know all about that. You're a
freak."
"You fuckin' cunt Avrail."

8:30am. The alarm clock
triggers its quadraphonic
jangle, ricochets off the walls
and splices into my brain like
a swarm of hot bullets. I
throw it against the wall but
it continues. At 9:17 I flick
the radio on to hear 'Up the
junction'. I wade through the
wavebands and run ashore on
the news station. USA v Haiti
didn't happen. My toothache
has gone.
There are dog ends on the
table and on the floor. I wear
the same suit. I have no
cigarettes.
I am scared.

I may have killed my little
sister yesterday afternoon. I
slashed her neck open with a
pint glass. Blood spurted over
Grandma who just stared.
I hear screams. I hear gurgling
noises.
I ran out of the restaurant.
Nobody followed me.
I got a cab home, done a
runner on the driver. I dug
out the family photo album,
took it over the park and
burned it.
Nobody came. Have I killed
her?
I spent the evening watching
'It's a wonderful life' and
ringing chatlines.
"What song has the line 'Bless
my cotton socks I'm in the
news' in?"
"I don't know. Do you want
to know what colour knickers
I'm wearing?"
"No. Sorry, goodbye."
Still nobody came.
I had bad dreams.
I dreamed that Dad had a
heart attack at a Blues game.
He was the only one in the
stadium and died alone.
I dreamed that Avrail died in
a car crash, her head
decapitated.
I dreamed of dead babies.
"Why hasn't anyone come?"
You can kill your own sister
and nobody cares.
It's 11:58. A knock at the
door.

THE END

the living room

HOME GAME Fraser Addecott
is a student in Southampton.

SUNDANCE TERMINAL
Martin Messent lives in Brighton

PLASTIC, THE ANIMATED, PING PONG GAME
Adam j Maynard published some of his writing in
shiny, a zine inspired by tv and plastic toys

STONE
Ralph Mepham

THE WHITE TRUNK STORY
Justin Cooke is a mystery on
the end of a mobile number.

HOUSE OF CHAINS Julia Brosnan lives in Manchester.
Her non-fiction book ***DETONATING THE NUCLEAR FAMILY***
is published by Scarlet Press.

RUSH: A LONG WAY FROM H Caroline Bergvall
writes text for performance and installation,
and teaches at Dartington College of Arts.

WAILING WALL
Jacqueline Lucas Palmer

FREEDOM CITY Michael Onile-Ere has written a novel
FREEDOM CITY from which this extract is taken.

Deborah Levy wrote ***SWALLOWING GEOGRAPHY***
and ***BEAUTIFUL MUTANTS*** (Vintage). Her new
novel ***BILLY & GIRL*** will appear later this year.

ABOUT LISA Tim Etchells writes for Forced Entertainment, a theatre group based in Sheffield.

HEAT Tim Hutchinson lives in London and works as an illustrator.

ROOTING Robyn Conway, is assistant editor of **PULP FACTION**.

FLUENCY Eva Forrai lives in Brixton

4 GOBLINS IN HAMBURGER GRAVY Duncan McLean lives in Scotland. He wrote ***BUNKER MAN***, soon to be reissued by Vintage.

EL FNA Joe Ambrose half lives in Morocco. Bits of this story are on the CD **10%** which features William Burroughs, Tim Simenon and others, on the Sub Rosa label.

HOMELANDS Mark Delaware claims (admits?) to have been working through his Madonna obsession for 12 years.

STILL LIFE WITH AN IDEA OF A TRAILER PARK Jay Merrill is working on a novel ***BEING DELIA***.

TEUTONIC PLATES Mark Love plays guitar, sings and is co-authoring a graphic novel.

THE PROMISE OF SWEET THINGS Jemma Kennedy works for a dodgy Soho film company

COME ON YOU BLUES Ralph Dartford lives in Essex.

WE GOT DEEP Amanda Gazidis. Please contact Pulp Faction.

SKIN

Abrasive new work from authors including Barry Adamson, ex-THE BAD SEEDS.

"Abusive, compelling imagery and ideas" TIME OUT

Fiction £5.99
1995, 128pp
ISBN 1899571000

TECHNOPAGAN

Among the writers are Jeff Noon, Sonya Aurora Madan, Steve Aylett, Nicholas Royle and Scanner.

"Technopagan describes a weird fucked-up country. A land of boogie cops, increased leisure citizens, bad sex and good drugs." WIRED

Fiction £6.99 1995, 128pp ISBN 1899571019

THE LIVING ROOM

(re-titled from 'Homelands') work from many new writers plus some you may have read before: Deborah Levy and Scottish author Duncan McLean.

Pulp Faction shows that "literary life on these shores does extend beyond Irvine Welsh." SELECT

Fiction £6.99. 1996, 128pp. ISBN 1899571027

F I S S I O N

Division of cells etc as a mode of reproduction; splitting of heavy atomic nucleus with release of energy –bomb.

"Bizarre & visionary."
THE GUARDIAN

Fiction £6.99
late summer 1996 128pp
ISBN 1899571035

S U B M I S S I O N S
DEADLINE 15 JUNE

Our next book, working title Random Factor, due in autumn 96, will be an unthemed collection in which writers and artists explore contemporary topics of importance to them. Texts from 750 to 3,000 words will be considered. Please submit one story only, on double-spaced A4 typescript. Response/return of typescripts is possible only if sae/postage provided.

Send text and/or images to:

RANDOM FACTOR,
Pulp Faction,
60 Alexander Road,
London, N19 3PQ

SKIN UP WITH FREE PULP OFFER

Subscribe to *PULP Faction* for 3 books
and receive 3 books delivered post-free to any UK
address˟, PLUS a *free* copy of *SKIN* (while stocks last).

I enclose a cheque payable to *PULP Faction* for:

☐ £18.00 Subscription: 3 titles starting with
....(specify)
plus a *free* copy of SKIN

☐ £5.99 SKIN

☐ £6.99 TECHNOPAGAN

☐ £6.99 HOMELANDS

☐ £6.99 FISSION

Name ....

Address ....

Postcode ....

Return to: PULP faction, BooksDirect,
60 Alexander Road,
London, N19 3PQ.
˟Orders from outside the EC, add £1.50 p&p per book or £4 per subscription.
US customers may order by credit card from AK Press on 415 923 1429.